ISLAND

Robert Sutherland

cover by
Bernard Leduc

Property of English Department
St. Peter Catholic High School

Scholastic Canada Ltd.

Scholastic Canada Ltd.
123 Newkirk Road, Richmond Hill, Ontario, Canada L4C 3G5

Scholastic Inc.
555 Broadway, New York, NY 10012, USA

Ashton Scholastic Pty Limited
PO Box 579, Gosford, NSW 2250, Australia

Ashton Scholastic Limited
Private Bag 94407, Greenmount, Auckland, New Zealand

Scholastic Publications Ltd.
Villiers House, Clarendon Avenue, Leamington Spa,
Warwickshire CV32 5PR, UK

Canadian Cataloguing in Publication Data

Sutherland, Robert, 1925-
 Death Island

ISBN 0-590-24190-7

I. Title.

PS8587.U85D43 1994   jC813'.54   C94-931537-0
PZ7.S88De 1994

Copyright © 1994 by Robert Sutherland. All rights reserved.
No part of this publication may be reproduced or stored in a
retrieval system, or transmitted in any form or by any means,
electronic, mechanical, recording, or otherwise, without written
permission of the publisher, Scholastic Canada Ltd., 123 Newkirk
Road, Richmond Hill, Ontario, Canada L4C 3G5. In the case of
photocopying or other reprographic copying, a licence must be
obtained from CANCOPY (Canadian Reprography Collective), 6
Adelaide Street East, Suite 900, Toronto, Ontario M5C 1H6.

7 6 5 4 3 2   Printed in Canada   5 6 7 8/9

Other Scholastic titles by this author:

Son of the Hounds
Suddenly a Spy

The Sandy and David mysteries:

The Mystery of Black Rock Island
The Loon Lake Murders
The Ghost of Ramshaw Castle

For Emily and Rhona:
instead of "Devil Lake."

1

The cry came on the high breath of the wind; came, lingered for a moment, then was gone, lost in the crash of waves on the rocky shore.

"Sandy!" His voice was hoarse, little more than a whisper. It was lost in the maelstrom of wind and lashing rain.

"Sandy!" But she was gone, back into the writhing darkness.

He stared into the murk but could see only the white tops of the driven waves and the towering spray of the sea dashing against the lurking rocks. He turned, hitching the collar of his oilskin higher.

"Sandy! Where are you?"

"Here, Davie." Over where they had tied the boat to the decrepit wharf. He moved carefully across the slippery rocks, heather clutching at his ankles, and slid down the slope to the shore.

Even here in comparative shelter the sea was

agitated, the boat rocking crazily, straining at the bow and stern lines. Sandy glanced up at him.

"Just checking. I think it'll be all right."

"Good." His hand closed on her rain-slick arm. "I thought I heard a noise back there. A cry. Someone calling. Out to sea."

"Someone calling?" The light of her flashlight touched his face. His eyes were large, his face white, anxious. "It couldn't be. There's no one out there tonight. It was just the wind."

"Yes of course. Just the wind." But he wasn't convinced.

"Come on, Davie," she said. "We have to find shelter. We'll try that way." She pointed.

"All right." But he held back, still listening.

She turned the light up again for a moment, catching the look on his face.

"I tell you it's just the wind. It makes strange sounds, you know. Sometimes it's like a mermaid crying. Or a lost child. But it's just the wind."

"Yes, yes, I know — " He stopped. There it was again — like a mermaid crying, or a lost child. Not from seaward this time, but from which direction? "There. Did you hear it?"

"Yes, I heard." She stopped, turning the light this way and that. But the beam went nowhere, swallowed by the Stygian blackness of the night. "It's just the wind." She said it again, but perhaps her voice lacked its former conviction. "Come on, Davie. There's the ruins of a blackhouse here somewhere."

He let her lead the way, scrambling up the slick slope, the wind clutching at them, the rain like a wet blanket around them. He could see nothing beyond her black shape but the small circle of light from her flashlight moving ahead of them.

"Is it far to this shelter?" he asked hopefully.

"No. . . . " She stopped so that he was beside her. "Maybe I should qualify that. It wasn't far last time I was here but that was in bright sunshine and I could see where I was going." She was casting the light about. "If we can find a burn — a creek — and follow that it will lead us to the — " She stopped abruptly. There was an indistinct sound off to their left, a sudden movement in the darkness. Something vaguely white was coming towards them. Sandy grabbed David's arm, swinging the light around, stepping back against him.

For a moment they could see nothing, then suddenly there was a black face surrounded by white wool, gentle eyes blinking.

"Holy smoke!" muttered David, shaken. "A sheep. You can't get away from these beasts in the Highlands, can you — even out here. But I thought you said this island is uninhabited."

"It is. I should have known." She laughed, uncertainly. "The sheep are left here to pasture. The owner leaves them except in lambing or shearing times. I know him. Archie MacDonald. He comes to check on them occasionally, I expect.

But generally they run wild. There must be more of them around, so we won't be taken by surprise next time. Where is that burn? It can't be far because it empties back there, near where we left the boat."

"Perhaps we should go back and start again — follow it right from the start. We won't get any wetter than we are now."

"If we have to. . . . Listen!" There was that sound again, a cry infinitely sad and lingering. David shivered involuntarily.

"It's just the wind," he reminded himself — and her.

This time she shook her head. "Something has been disturbed. Seals, maybe, or birds. Let me see now." She paused to reconnoitre. "We came this way so the burn *must* be over there. Come on." He followed her obediently and a few moments later they were rewarded. They came upon a stream tumbling down the slope.

"Now, we follow it. We'll come to the cottage sooner or later. It's beside the burn."

They were climbing again, heads bent against the rain, oilskin hats pulled down, feet thrusting against tenacious undergrowth, stumbling over sudden clefts and protuberances. David could distinguish the crown of the hill now, a faint demarcation against the sky. It seemed to recede before them as they climbed until he wondered if they would ever reach it.

They did, at last, though it didn't seem to

make much difference. He still could see nothing. But he heard a new sound now, a distant, booming reverberation, like continuous thunder.

"What's that?"

"That's the sea in the caves and tunnels. It's pretty wild on a night like this. I'll show you tomorrow. We haven't far to go now." He still couldn't see anything but she was stepping out with new confidence. And a few minutes later he saw a blacker shape looming out of the night. Sandy caught it in the glow from her flashlight; the stone walls of an ancient bothy, with vacant windows and no door. She shone the light up and he saw that most of the roof had fallen. But at one end it seemed to be intact.

"This way. You know the old saying, 'any port in a storm'. And I think you'll find this better than it looks."

They stepped across the doorstep onto a dirt floor. "This end was the byre," she said. "Where they kept the cattle. She shone the light on another stone wall dividing the house in two. There was a door here, a shapeless slab hanging drunkenly on rusty hinges. She pushed it open. "Come away ben," she invited, "into the luxurious living quarters."

It had never been luxurious, of course, but he could see that it might once have been warm and comfortable. There had been a wooden floor at one time, and glass in the tiny windows. There was still a fireplace in the end wall, under the part of the roof that was still whole.

"We'll be dry anyway." Sandy's light moved quickly around the room. "Archie MacDonald probably comes here if he's caught out in a storm, like we were. See, there's straw on the floor, and peat for burning, and maybe a lamp. . . . " The light moved along the wall above the hearth. "Yes. There it is. And matches." In a moment the soft glow of a paraffin lamp cheered them while the wind battered against the stout stone walls and the rain pelted down into the roofless part beyond.

"Now for a fire, and a cup of tea," said Sandy cheerfully. "If there's a light and matches and peat to burn there's sure to be some tea here somewhere. Let's — " she stopped abruptly. She was staring into the grate. "Davie . . . Look at that."

"What? What is it?"

"Smoke! See it?" Sure enough a curl of smoke drifted up from the ashes of the previous fire. She stretched out her hand towards it.

"It's still warm!" She looked up at him, puzzled. "Someone's been here not too long ago."

"Probably the shepherd you mentioned," reasoned David. "Caught in the sudden storm, like us."

"Then where is he now?"

"Gone, I guess. Back home. His boat's gone, hasn't it? Or would he park it somewhere other than where we tied up?"

She shook her head. "That's the only place, as far as I know. Certainly the only shelter in a storm. You're right. He must have come out to check on his sheep, lit a fire, then decided to go back before the storm got worse. . . ."

He looked at her curiously. "You don't sound convinced."

"I'm not," she admitted. "Archie's no seaman. I think he would sooner have stayed here until the storm blew itself out. If he *did* leave, he would head straight for home — and we saw no sign of him."

"So — what are you saying?"

"I don't know." She was silent for a moment. She removed her oilskin hat, shaking the rain off it. Then she shrugged. "The boat's gone, so I guess he left. I just hope he made it."

"Well, we're here for the night." David took the packet of sandwiches from his pocket and tossed his oilskin into the corner. "Let's get a fire going."

That took only a few minutes. Soon the kindling was blazing, and then came the sweet smell of burning peat. Sandy found a kettle already filled with water and set it close to the fire.

The flame in the lamp flickered, as a gust of wind found its way through some unseen hole in the wall; flickered, guttered, and went out. But the light from the fire was all they needed. David watched shadow and light dancing across the walls while the elements raged outside, and he shook his head in bemused wonder.

"We get ourselves into the weirdest predicaments, don't we," he mused. "No one will be worried if we don't show up tonight, will they?"

"No, we're not expected until tomorrow." Back at Ramshaw Castle, where Sandy was a tour guide and David was employed as a handyman for the summer. With two days off, he and Sandy had left the castle, driven to Stornoway and set out in a small but eminently seaworthy boat for a few hours on the water. The weather forecast had been good, but no meteorologist had yet solved the riddle of the sudden storms that made the Minch one of the most treacherous of the coastal waters around the British Isles. They had given up trying to batter their way home against rising seas and, with the onset of night, had found shelter on this small, rocky island, with its high spine rising to cliffs of columnar basalt.

"It should calm down soon enough for us to be back before we're missed," Sandy continued. "The water's beginning to boil. There should be mugs here somewhere."

"One, anyway." David had found a cracked, handle-less mug, none too clean. "We'll have to take turns with it. What are you going to brew the tea in?"

"In the mug, I suppose. I don't see a teapot anywhere. . . . "

They had a picnic of sorts, munching on thick

meat sandwiches and taking turns sipping from the mug. They had a long night ahead of them, David reflected, but they were comfortable enough, even though they were only just beyond the reach of the raging elements. They both wore heavy fisherman's sweaters, and with the fire the chill night air would be no problem. They had been in worse spots than this, both here in the Hebrides and back home in the wilds of Algonquin Park. Compared to those, this was a mild adventure indeed.

David looked across at Sandy. She had been raised in the Hebrides, living a good part of her life on her uncle's trawler, so she knew these islands and waters. She was at home, squatting there before the hearth, the light from the fire on her face and in her red-gold curls. And it was reflected in her disturbingly blue eyes when she looked at him — eyes that he realized were troubled and anxious.

"What is it?" he asked.

"I don't know — " She sat for a moment, still and listening. He could hear only the wind and the rain, and the distant surf. "I don't know. But there's something wrong. . . . "

2

David awakened to see myriad dust particles dancing in the sun's rays, which streamed in through the tiny window and the gap above, where the roof should have been. Through the gap he could see white clouds moving across a blue sky.

He closed his eyes and lay still for a moment, listening. He could still hear the wind — a mere whisper compared to the night before — and the booming of the surf. And close at hand, the crackle of the fire. Sandy must have relit it. He had noticed in the night that it was on the point of dying, but he had been too sleepy to do anything about it. He had pulled the oilskin over his head and gone back to sleep.

Now he pushed it aside and sat up. The kettle was there by the fire, steaming promisingly. But there was no other sign of Sandy. He moved the kettle back from the fire, pulled on his boots and went outside.

Although the rain had ceased and the wind had eased, from the doorway he could see great white-capped combers rolling in, breaking in thunderous tumult on the rocky shore.

"I guess we won't be going anywhere for a while," he thought. "Now where's Sandy?"

It was as if she heard him. "David! I'm up here."

She had climbed the hill above the cottage, and was waving and beckoning to him. In a few moments he had joined her, and looked around in delight.

The view was unlimited this morning. Looking westward beyond the tossing breakers David could see the hills of Harris, hunching into the sky; in the opposite direction, the monolithic mountains stood sentinel over West Sutherland. Scattered islands were etched sharp and clear against sea and sky. Away to the north a ferry bucked its way toward Harris.

At his feet heather, yellow buttercups and purple vetch moved before the breath of the wind like another sea. And high in the air over the northern cliffs the sea birds wheeled and called, or soared on outstretched wings.

"Magnificent!" breathed David. "Absolutely magnificent! Although that wind is still a bit fresh. How long, d'you think, before we can shove off?"

Sandy looked doubtful. "A few hours," she guessed. "We're here till noon anyway. Maybe longer."

"And us without any breakfast. Too bad I don't like mutton." He had spotted several sheep grazing nearby. "Well, at least we have tea. *You'll* be happy, anyway."

She laughed. "I've always said, as long as you have tea you've nothing to worry about. Stick around and you'll come to agree with me — some day." She caught his arm and they started back to the house. "And after our cup of tea, I'll show you why this island is known as 'the whale'."

David stopped and looked around. "That's easy. It looks like a whale on the surface — a humpback whale."

"There's more to it than that. You'll see."

A half-hour later they were hiking north along the ridge. They could hear again the echoing roar they had heard the night before, more subdued, but increasing as they advanced. They crossed another hill and a new vista opened up. On a headland high above the sea old stone works outlined an ancient courtyard, and a tower stood, square and solid, poised on the edge of the precipice.

"Sgarbeg Castle," said Sandy. "A stronghold of the MacLeans. Abandoned centuries ago, of course. This way."

They crossed a natural causeway to the plateau that had once been a forecourt. She led him to the low wall beside the ancient keep. "Look."

From here they could see past a deep inlet that almost cut the island in two, to towering cliffs of columnar basalt, like the pipes of an organ. The pounding seas had carved out caves and tunnels, with vaulted arches here and there framing the flying spume. The cliff sides were colour-splashed with orange lichen and pink and white campion, and all around the sea birds swarmed, calling and crying. Down below on boulder-fields of collapsed columns, seals lazed in the sun, just beyond the reach of the lashing seas.

Then, without a word, Sandy pointed beyond the inlet. There, suddenly and seemingly out of solid ground, a great geyser of water exploded high into the air. The column of water seemed to hang for a moment, glistening in the sun, then fell back, while the spray was whipped away in the wind.

"What in the world!" David stared in fascination. "What caused *that*?"

"Come. I'll show you."

They had rounded the inlet and were climbing to the highest point of the island when it happened again. This time David was aware of a rushing roar, of the ground trembling beneath his feet. Then there it was, just ahead: a sudden, towering fountain, there for a moment, then gone, while the spray from it wrapped around them.

"We're standing over a cave," Sandy explained. "On a day like this the waves come barreling in and smash against the back wall of the cave. They have to go somewhere. There's a fissure in the rock here, so — that's the result."

"I see. So that's what you meant — when it happens it looks like a whale blowing. . . . " He felt the ground shaking beneath his feet again, and a roar like an approaching express train. "Come on. We don't need another shower." They stepped back hastily, and watched the next waterspout shoot up, painting a rainbow in the air. "Can we see the mouth of the cave you're talking about?"

"Perhaps. We'll have a look. But be careful. There are no guardrails up here."

They approached the edge of the cliff carefully, then lay on their stomachs to look over. Birds erupted at their approach, guillemots, shags and puffins launching out from shelves and pinnacles, while clouds of kittiwakes screamed in protest.

And down below on the rock-strewn shoreline they saw something that caused them to forget the cave. Something moved down there, at the whim of the waves. It came in on the torn crests, hung there, then was sucked away and swallowed; only to be regurgitated and come back, to hit the rocks, smash into pieces and go out, again and again, as if it were the plaything of a careless monster.

"What is it?" wondered David. "A boat — or what's left of it. D'you suppose it's a recent casualty?"

"It's recent." Sandy's voice was grim. "*Very*

recent, Davie. It's . . . " Suddenly she was grabbing his arm. "Davie! Oh dear God! Look there!"

He looked to where she was pointing, and saw it: the broken body of a man, wedged between two boulders. Splayed arms and legs moved obscenely at the pull of the backwash.

David sucked in his breath sharply, his hand closing on Sandy's. "He's dead," he whispered, after a moment. There could be no doubt of that. "Do you think it's — the shepherd?"

"Yes. It's Archie. That must have been his boat. The foolish man!"

"What should we do?" wondered David. "We can't just leave him there."

"There's nothing we *can* do — except notify the police. We're not cliff climbers and no boat is going to go close inshore in that surf. Come on. We'd better go back to the boat and radio for help."

They pushed back from the edge, stood up and started back in subdued silence, hand in hand.

"I don't understand," said Sandy at last. "It doesn't make sense. What was the man thinking of?"

"It seems plain enough," said David, gently. "He didn't want to wait out the storm. Perhaps there was a very good reason why he had to get back home. And you said he's not a very good sailor."

"But, he wasn't stupid either. All he had to do was go around the south of the island. That's the easiest way — the shortest way. I'm sure that's how he always comes. So what was he doing up near those cliffs? *That's* what doesn't make sense."

She stopped suddenly. They were standing on the grounds of the ancient castle, looking back at the precipitous crags.

"Davie, there's something wrong about this." She started walking again. "When we get a chance we're going to come back here, you and I. To find out what it is."

3

"So — what do you think, Davie?" Sandy leaned on the low wall, chin in hand, watching David trying to decide which of the green shoots in the garden were weeds and which were flowers. She had just conducted a group of tourists around the castle, and was wearing her uniform — a white blouse and tartan kilt. She was a MacLeod herself, but today she wore the ancient Morrison tartan in honour of the original owners of Ramshaw Castle.

"I think," said David, "that the only way to be sure is to pull everything up. Clean it right out. Then anything that comes up *has* to be a weed."

Sandy laughed. She laughed a lot, and he liked to see it; her face lit up and her eyes danced.

"That wasn't what I meant," she said. "I mean about Archie Macdonald. Do you think I'm just imagining that there's a mystery?"

"Probably." David stood up, brushing off his knees. "After all the adventures we've been through together you look for another one every time something odd happens. And ten-to-one there's a simple explanation. Although," he added, "finding a body *is* pretty unusual."

"So what's the simple explanation?"

"*I* don't know. The answer probably lies in the fact that he was a poor sailor. He decided he had to go home in spite of the worsening weather — there could be any number of reasons for that. I don't suppose we'll ever know what it was. He lost control of his boat, and ended up — where we found him."

Sandy shook her head stubbornly. "I keep telling you, Davie, that if he'd been heading home he couldn't possibly have ended up there. The seas would have carried him onto the rocks off the *south* coast. And if he missed those he would have ended up on the Long Island somewhere."

"So he took the long way. Or maybe he wasn't going home at all. Maybe one of the sheep fell off the cliff and he went to rescue it."

"In that weather?" Sandy sighed. "You don't know anything about the sea, do you, Davie? I suppose you don't have many hurricane winds or gale-force waves pounding away at your home in Woodstock, Ontario."

"We had a tornado once," said David, defensively. "But no. I love the sea but I don't know much about it."

"Well, I can tell you that even the best of sailors wouldn't have gone looking for a lost sheep in that weather, near those rocks."

"Okay," acknowledged David. "There's a mystery. I still think there must be a simple explanation. We just don't know what it is. And as far as I can see we aren't likely to find out, either."

"But we can try — can't we?"

David regarded the determined tilt of her chin and grinned.

"Of course we could," he said. "I suppose you have some idea how we could go about it?"

"No," she admitted. "I haven't any specific plans. But first of all we have to go back out to Sgarbeg Island — to 'the scene of the crime'. We can go on from there."

"Do we hire a boat again? I don't know about you, but the last time just about cleaned me out."

"No, we don't have to. Alec MacAllister is going out Friday with his lobster boat to bring Archie's sheep back. We can go with him. I've already asked and he's quite willing."

"Friday? That's my day off but you're supposed to work, aren't you?"

"I can exchange with Jeannie. She owes me one."

"But if we're rounding up and loading sheep we won't have much time to go sleuthing, will we?"

"Oh, he's not expecting us to help with that. He has a man and a dog — regular crew. First, we'll load any of Archie's personal things we can find — the kettle, the tea, the peat and so forth.

We'll bring that back for his wife — that'll give us an excuse to talk to her. I want to see what *she* thinks could have happened. Then we'll borrow Alec's dinghy and go up to the cliffs. We have to see them from the sea. We have to go where Archie went."

"Then I hope the weather's good. I don't fancy ending up the same way he did."

"Oh, don't worry about that. Alec's only going if it's reasonably calm."

"Reasonably calm?" David was doubtful. "What some of you people call reasonably calm I would call a gale. But it sounds like fun. . . ."

* * *

"Do you go to the island often?" David was standing beside the skipper of the *Maisie* as the stubby boat rode the long swell easily, the mast tracing a lazy arc across the sky.

"To Sgarbeg?" Alec MacAllister shook his head. There was a dead pipe clutched between his teeth, jutting from his weather-beaten face. His pale blue eyes were fixed on the whale-back shape of the island looming ahead. "No one goes to Sgarbeg if they can help it."

"No one . . . ?" David looked expectantly at the skipper, but apparently no further enlightenment was to be forthcoming. He glanced across at Sandy. She too was mystified. "I don't understand," he prompted. "Why don't people go to Sgarbeg?"

Alec moved the pipe from his mouth, knocked the upturned bowl against the binnacle, then returned it to his mouth and blew through it. A little puff of dottle erupted into the air and was swept away in the breeze.

"They have another name for the island — did you know?" He glanced at Sandy, his eyebrows raised a fraction.

She shook her head. "Unless you mean — Whale Island?"

He shook his head in turn, impatiently. "No, not that. Never mind . . . Of course if you're *paid* to go, you go. But not else."

"You're not being paid this time," Sandy pointed out.

"No. This is different. I'm going for a friend." He adjusted the wheel a fraction, heading the bow towards the south end of the island. "I was paid to go to Sgarbeg once — two years ago, just about. And it was very near the death of me."

"Why? What happened?"

"There was a cargo vessel, the *Neptune*. She was a small one, not more than three thousand tons. Out of Venezuela, I believe with a mixed cargo; heading for Liverpool by way of New York. Hurricane winds drove her away off course. She came around the Butt of Lewis and down the Minch. The storm was too much for her. Her rudder was carried away so she was at the mercy of the sea. She called for assistance but there were a lot of ships in distress that day, and

21

nothing that could weather such a storm was near enough to come to her aid. She was driven onto the rocks and cliffs at the north end of Sgarbeg Island."

The island lay just ahead of them now, low at the southern end, climbing to towering cliffs in the north.

"A section of her bow was sighted in the morning on the rocks, but by the time anyone got there even that had sunk and she was gone. They found a bit of wreckage and three bodies but that was it. There were no survivors."

There were a number of ships in sight today, taking advantage of the relative calm. Several fishing boats were engaged in their trade; one of MacBrayne's ferries made its way to the outer isles, and a graceful motor-sailer had white sails set to catch the easy breeze. The smiling sea moved gently with latent power, biding its time.

"And you — how were you involved?" asked David.

"Well, a salvage crew came up from Liverpool, you see. They wanted to save as much of the cargo as they could. I don't know how successful they were. But when they were near done they had engine trouble on the tug and she had to go back for repairs. There was a forecast of bad weather so they wanted to finish up as soon as possible. They asked for the use of my *Maisie* for the last day. We anchored off the cliffs above the wreck and the divers — there were only two left — were going down and bringing up mostly personal stuff from the crew's quarters for the families."

He eased the wheel to skirt around a welter of spray where the swell broke over a scatter of rocks. They were rounding the southern tip of the island.

"Then something strange happened. I was down below having a pipe and a nip — just a wee one, you understand — when there seemed to be some excitement up top. Of course it was none of my business, so I finished my pipe, but after a wee while I came up to look around.

"I just stepped out on the deck when I was fetched a fearful dunt on the back of the head." He rubbed that area ruefully. "I tell you I saw shooting stars, exploding rockets and roman candles, then nothing at all. When I woke up I was on my bunk. The cabin was all fuzzy and going around like a whirligig and there was a lump on my head the size of a football. One of the divers was there, soaking me with a towel and looking mighty anxious indeed. I tell you, lad, getting knocked out is nought like what you see on the telly. Your hero gets smashed on the head with a gun butt and he's out for maybe five minutes then he's up and after the bad guys like nothing's happened." Alec shook his head and winced as if he could still feel the pain. "Maybe I'm getting old, but it wasn't that way with me. Those divers had to sail my *Maisie* home for me and the doctor kept me in bed for a week."

"But — what happened? Who hit you?"

"Who? Och, no. Nobody hit me. It was an accident. Those men were divers but they were no sailors. One of their knots on the guy rope slipped and the boom swung round and hit me. They were fair scunnert, I can tell you. Paid me triple what I'd agreed to so it was worth the pain — though I wasn't so sure about that at the time."

The skipper's eyes swept the length of the island, and he frowned.

"Oh aye, it was an accident. But accidents seem to happen out here more than they should. Look at what happened to Archie. No, lad, yon is a good place to steer clear of. We'll not be staying any longer today than we have to to get Archie's sheep off. . . ."

4

It didn't take Sandy and David long to gather up
the few belongings Archie MacDonald had left behind. A careful search disclosed nothing new, and
with the help of a wheelbarrow found behind the
house they loaded everything, including two bar-
row loads of peat, on the deck of the *Maisie*.

The sheep were scattered widely over the island, and even with the help of the wise old collie,
rounding them up promised to be a lengthy proc-
ess. Leaving dog and man to it, David slipped the
dinghy from its tow, and Sandy started the outboard.

They left the small cove and turned northward. Here the cliffs were low, the swell breaking
against them in a long line of white water, the
ground behind rising to the whale-back ridge.
Soon the rock wall rose higher, climbing to the
headland capped by the ancient 'donjon,' or castle
keep.

"I want to get a good picture of this." David slipped the camera from its case, studied the scene for a moment, then shook his head. "I need something else in the foreground besides water. I know. Head out to sea for a minute, Sandy. That way I can get you in the picture too."

She obediently swung the craft seaward, and he framed the picture in the viewfinder. Sandy was there, laughing, the wind tossing her sunlit hair.

"Perfect." He snapped the picture, then shook his head again. "Maybe that wasn't such a good idea. With you in the foreground who's going to look at a heap of old stones?"

"Flattery will get you everywhere," grinned Sandy. She pointed ahead before swinging the dinghy back on course. "*That* would make a good picture too."

The motor-sailer was approaching them obliquely, white sails set to catch the breeze, a small bow wave creaming back along her flanks.

"Yeah. She's a beauty." He studied the gleaming white ship on the turquoise sea for a moment, then took the picture. "It looks like they appreciate beauty too," he said, lowering his camera. "There's a man at the rail watching you through binoculars."

"Watching *me*? Och away! He's looking at the castle. Everyone takes pictures of Sgarbeg Castle. Mr. Cuomo must be entertaining again."

"Why do you say that? Who is Mr. Cuomo?"

"He owns that yacht — the *Kittiwake*. And since he's been sailing the Minch for two years he's not likely to be looking at the scenery himself. He'll have guests aboard. No doubt they're comparing Sgarbeg to Staffa." She was referring to the famous basalt island with its hugh caves. "Staffa has higher cliffs and bigger caves, but it doesn't have a castle."

"It doesn't blow like a whale either," mused David. "I suppose its caves are *too* big for that."

"Aye, that's right. . . . "

They passed below the castle and nosed into the inlet that almost cut the island in two. The sound of the little outboard was suddenly magnified, echoing off the rock walls on either side. Birds launched from their nests on innumerable ledges, shrieking and crying in protest at being disturbed, milling about in great agitated circles above where their droppings lay like snow on the shelves and whitewashed the sheer precipices.

Sandy eased back on the throttle so the clamour subsided and they drifted along while the swell slapped against the walls and swilled back and forth in the confines of the chasm.

David sat in the bow, taking more pictures, until the walls closed in ahead, and Sandy swung the dinghy around and headed back out to sea. David noticed, as they emerged, that the *Kittiwake* was still in sight, angled away from them now as she tacked against the wind.

They headed north again, and soon they were

below the towering rock columns. The cliff face itself seemed to be alive with the restless movements of nested puffins, guillemots and razorbills. Where the rock was visible it glowed with lichen and campion. And at the foot of the crags lay the boulder-fields where cormorants were draped over the rocks, wings spread out as if to dry. Grey Atlantic seals watched their approach warily, ready to slip into the safety of the water at a moment's notice.

Here and there the eternally restless sea had pounded perfect arches through outcroppings of rock, and along the shoreline where the swell swept in to break in jewelled spume, several cave mouths yawned.

Sandy cut back on the motor, maintaining just enough way to hold them poised off shore. She pointed high overhead.

"That's where we looked over and saw Archie's body. And the body was just over there."

There was only a seal there now, sleeping peacefully.

"Which is the cave that causes the waterspout?"

"That one." She indicated the largest opening. "The waves aren't big enough to spout today. Although when the tide comes in it might happen. Shall we go in?"

"Sure, if you think it's safe. You're the captain."

Sandy turned the dinghy towards the opening.

Now the swell caught them and David grabbed the gunwales in alarm as they were swept ahead with frightening speed. But Sandy was ready. She shifted into reverse so that the propeller countered the thrust of the sea and they eased gently into the cave.

Then a giant hand caught them. In the confined space, the swell, as if suddenly alarmed, flung itself against the rock walls in a fury of spray, surged forward against the invisible inner wall, and came back in a tidal wave, tossing the dinghy, showering its crew with spume. The walls and ceiling, meeting somewhere in the gloom overhead, formed an echo chamber that amplified the sounds of the battling outboard and the tumult of the frustrated waves.

David looked back in consternation, but Sandy had obviously expected nothing less. He grinned in relief. She was enjoying the challenge of manoeuvering the dinghy in a sea that was trying to hurl them in opposite directions at the same time.

When David turned to look around he was startled to see seals lying peacefully on ledges higher than his head, ignoring the turmoil about them. He raised his camera, wiping the spray from the lens, and aimed it in their direction, steadying himself as best he could against the plunging of the boat. The flash split the gloom once, twice. He hoped, doubtfully, that the results would be worthwhile.

He was about to try a third shot when a sudden violent movement of the dinghy threw him off balance and onto the floor boards. He struggled up, clutching the gunwale. A dark shape, huge and black, surged through the water beside them. David stared in apprehension as it bumped against the boat, then disappeared. It suddenly loomed up in front of them: a seal, a big bull seal, head and chest out of the water, challenging them to go any further.

Sandy refused the challenge. She opened the throttle and the dinghy surged back, through the welter of spray where the inrushing swell met the backwash, into the bright sunlight. She pulled up, to idle offshore again. David caught his breath.

"That," he said, with feeling, "was one *big* seal."

She nodded. "It was, wasn't it. And I'll bet it was just as scared as we were. But it could easily have upset us and we don't need a ducking. Can you see how at high tide and with a running sea the water could be forced up through the crevice?"

"Oh yes. But how did those seals get up on the higher ledges? Do they leap out of the water like dolphins?"

"No. They went in at high tide and were stranded. They'll wait there for the tide to come in again. Do you think you got a picture of them?"

"I hope so. We'll have to wait and see though.

Well — here we are at the 'scene of the crime'. Does it give you any ideas?"

Sandy hesitated, then shook her head regretfully. "I'm afraid it doesn't. I was hoping — well, I don't quite know what I was hoping for. Why did Archie come here on a stormy night? I still haven't a clue. Take some more pictures, Davie — of the whole scene. Maybe looking at them later will give us an idea or two. Right now I suppose we should be getting back. Alec may be waiting for us."

"Perhaps," suggested David, "we could come back again when we have more time. We could stay in the old house — or bring a tent. Give ourselves time to explore the old castle as well as the caves. Some time when the sea is *really* calm. When we don't even have this swell to throw us about once we get in there."

Sandy nodded slowly. "Yes, we could do that. If we could arrange it pretty soon. You'll be going home before long. But I don't know what else we can do." She swung the dinghy around and headed back the way they had come.

They paid no heed to the *Kittiwake*. She was angled towards them again, and the man was still there at the rail with his binoculars.

* * *

"They're leaving." He lowered the glasses, a worried frown on his brow. "They took a lot of pictures. Including one in the cave. I swear I saw a flash."

His companion didn't share his concern. "Everyone takes pictures. Do you recognize them?"

"Yes. The girl anyway. She's Sandy MacLeod, from Ramshaw Castle. The boy must be her friend from Canada."

"Well, there you are. She's showing him the Hebrides and he's taking pictures to show the folks back home. What are you worried about?"

"Maybe it's nothing. But I don't like it. Those two kids who found the body are the same ones who sent Ramshaw to jail. First it'll be them nosing around, then before you know it someone with a badge will decide to take a closer look at MacDonald's 'accident'. We've got a good thing going here. We don't want a couple of kids to jeopardize it."

The other joined him at the rail and watched the departing dinghy. "Look, I told you — I've got everything under control. But if that's the way you feel we won't take any chances. We'll have them watched. If the worst happens we can always arrange a little incident for these two. But I'm sure it won't come to that."

5

She was a wee wisp of a woman. She sat on the edge of her chair — perhaps because if she sat any further back her feet would not touch the floor — and nervously twisted a handkerchief in her lap. She seemed lost in the castle room with its high, vaulted ceilings. "David, this is Mrs. MacDonald. Archie's wife." Sandy turned to the visitor to explain. "David was with me on Sgarbeg Island."

"How do you do," said David awkwardly. "I'm very sorry about what happened."

"Thank you," she said softly. "I didn't mean to disturb anyone. I just thought . . . "

"It's no trouble," Sandy assured her. "I'm glad you're here. We were going to see you tonight. And you came just at the right time. I'm between tours and David's on his break — aren't you, Davie. Mrs. MacAllister will bring us a cup of tea in a few minutes." She hesitated. "Is there any way we can help you, Mrs. MacDonald?"

"Oh my dear, you already have. Bringing Archie's things from — from that place. Alec told me I had you to thank for that. But please call me Jemmie. No one calls me Mrs. MacDonald. My name is Jemima, but no one calls me that either." She forced a smile that lingered only a moment. "I know your uncle very well, Sandy. He is an old friend of Archie's. *Was*, I suppose I should say." Her hand closed convulsively on the handkerchief. "The police told me you found . . . Archie?"

"Yes. David and I were caught out on the Minch when the storm blew up, and took shelter on Sgarbeg. We guessed Archie had been there, because the ashes in the hut were still warm. But we missed him. He had already left."

Mrs. MacDonald shook her head in bewilderment. "I can't understand why he left when the seas were running. He *always* stayed overnight if the weather was bad — sometimes longer. As long as necessary. He didn't like the sea. I wanted him to give up the grazing out there. It's an — an unlucky place. Always has been. But we haven't much land, and the rent was cheap . . . and now look what happened." She twisted her handkerchief in her hands. "We should have known. . . . "

Her voice trailed off. Sandy and David exchanged puzzled glances.

"What do you mean?" asked Sandy gently after a moment. "You should have known . . . ?"

"Oh — oh, nothing. I'm sorry. It's just that —

that I don't know what happened."

"There was no reason why he felt he *had* to get home?" suggested Sandy.

She shook her head. "Not that I know of. He would have told me if there were. There's something else. The police said he was found at the north end — where the cliffs are. Is that true?"

Sandy nodded. "David and I had climbed to the top of the cliffs and looked over. That's when we saw him — and the wreckage of his boat."

"I see." Then Jemmie MacDonald shook her head again. "No, I don't see at all. He wouldn't come home that way. I know. I've been out there with him. He always takes the shortest way possible. So why would he go up there — especially in bad weather? Unless he hit those rocks just off the south shore. If so, could the waves have carried him away up there?"

"No. Not a chance. He *must* have gone that way for some reason. Maybe there was someone else in danger and he went to help."

"That's what the police suggest. I suppose it's possible. Archie wasn't a good sailor but if someone needed help he wouldn't think of his own safety. But they haven't heard of anyone in trouble. No one seems to be missing. Surely if that was the case it would have been reported?"

"I don't know what to think," admitted Sandy. "I suppose as far as the police are concerned, it was accidental drowning?"

"Not drowning, no. It was a fractured skull

and internal injuries. From being thrown against the rocks, I expect. But yes, it was accidental death. I have no quarrel with that." She blinked back tears. "I would just like to know why he went — that way — in bad weather. I didn't think he'd been on the cliff side since the divers left the wreck."

"Wreck?" Sandy looked at her with new interest. "Would that be the wreck of the *Neptune*?"

"Aye, that's right. Archie used to go and watch the salvaging from the heights — never by boat, you see. He would just watch them from the cliffs. They recovered most of the cargo, I believe. Everything valuable, anyway. But that was almost two years ago."

Mrs. MacAllister, the castle cook, came in bearing a tray laden with tea and hot buttered scones, with a cold bottle of Irn Bru for David.

"Now Jemmie," she said kindly, "Here's a nice cup of tea to warm you. We're very sorry for your trouble, all of us. If there's anything we can do . . . I know that's what we always say at a time like this, but we really mean it." She poured out tea for Jemmie and Sandy and a cup for herself. "Was that the *Neptune* you were talking about when I came in? She went down off Sgarbeg in a storm."

Sandy nodded. "Your Alec was telling us about his part in the salvaging — and how he got hit on the head. It's funny, I can only recall it vaguely, yet it was only two years ago."

"There's a reason for that," nodded Mrs. Mac-Allister. "There were other ships bigger and more important than the *Neptune* in trouble that day. Especially the Dublin ferry."

"Of course! Now I remember. There were several ships lost in the Irish Sea, weren't there? And the ferry collided with another ship and lost quite a few passengers. *That's* what made the headlines. The *Neptune* was just a small tramp. You see, Mrs. MacAllister, she was wrecked on the north cliffs where we — where Archie was found. That's how the wreck came into the conversation."

"I see. Well, if he was up there in that storm, it's not surprising. . . . " She turned sympathetically to Jemmie. "What will you do, Jemmie? Is there insurance to help you out?"

"Yes, a little. I'll manage. Everyone's been so kind. I'll give up the grazing on Sgarbeg, of course. I never want to see that place again."

"I can understand that," said Sandy compassionately. "Actually Davie and I are thinking of going back some time, if we get some good weather. We want to explore the caves."

"Oh dear!" Jemmie looked distressed. "Do you really want to go back to that dreadful place?"

"Now Jemmie — they're young. Imagine! Exploring caves. Oh, to be young again. When you get to be our age caves are just cold, damp holes in the ground."

"And that waterspout!" Jemmie shivered. "It's

a cave that causes that, isn't it? I don't know why Archie was so interested in it."

"Oh? Was he?"

"Yes. I remember he once said there's more to it than meets the eye. I don't know what he meant by that."

David caught Sandy's eye, his eyebrows raised questioningly. She nodded almost imperceptibly.

"Is that all he said — that there's more to it than meets the eye?"

"Oh no — I think he said something else, I can't remember what. But not much else, mind you. He doesn't say much, does my Archie. He's a quiet man. Was, I should say." Tears welled up in her eyes. She dabbed at them fiercely with her handkerchief. "I must go. Thank you so much."

"But we haven't done anything," said Sandy, helplessly.

"Just talking helps." She put her teacup down, barely touched. "I'm sorry to be so — so weepy. My friends assure me it will get better over time."

"Just a minute. We'll give you a ride home."

"No, no, the walk will do me good. I need the fresh air."

"Then you'll take these scones with you." Mrs. MacAllister picked up the plate. "Just you wait. I'll package them for you."

"You're all so kind. . . ."

Sandy put her arm around the little woman. "I just wish we could do more," she said.

"Thank you. There's really nothing . . . " Jemmie MacDonald hesitated. "But I really would like to know why Archie was up there at those cliffs. . . . "

6

Three days later David's duties took him into town. He stopped at the butcher's shop first. It was very busy, so he left the order for the castle kitchen and was told to call back for it in about forty-five minutes. He then drove to the photographers, parked in front and went inside.

"There should be some pictures ready for McCrimmon," he said, producing his receipt.

The girl sifted through a rack of envelopes. "McCrimmon. Right. Here we are."

David paid her, took the envelope and slipped in to the cafe next door.

"Coffee and a doughnut please," he ordered. Then he opened the envelope.

The pictures were good, especially the ones in which he had managed to include Sandy. He went through them slowly: the columnar cliffs, the birds, the seals, the immaculate white *Kitti-wake*; even the two taken in the gloom of the cave.

He looked at these last two with special interest. They showed the swell breaking in white froth against the rock walls, reaching in vain for the seals on the ledges. Only one of the pictures had caught the higher ledge with its gray shape.

He finished his coffee and doughnut and left the cafe. He dropped the envelope of pictures in the open window of the car onto the passenger's seat. He was about to turn away when a voice hailed him.

"Hello! Young man!"

He turned. There was a man approaching, a burly, bearded man who moved with a decided limp.

"Yes? Can I help you?"

"I hope you can." The man leaned against the car, and appeared to be glad of the support. "Can you tell me where I might find a boat for hire?"

"Gee, I'm afraid not. I don't live here, you see. I'm just here for the summer, working out at Ramshaw Castle."

"Ah. American, are you?"

"No. Canadian. But maybe I know someone — two people, in fact — who could help you. There's Alec MacAllister . . . "

"Ah . . . the *Maisie*."

"That's right. You know him?"

"Och no." Something seemed to amuse the man. "But I've heard of him. Where can I find him?"

"I don't know where he lives, but his wife

works at the castle, and he comes to pick her up when she's through — soon after ten o'clock. He'll be there tonight. I could tell him to get in touch with you."

"Aye, well . . . you mentioned *two* people . . . ?"

"Yes. Sandy MacLeod. She's at the castle too. A guide. I know *she* knows where to hire a boat because she arranged one for us a few days ago. That was what you might call a self-drive. No driver included."

"Ah! That's just what I'm looking for. And this girl is at the castle too? Maybe I could come out there. In fact — I understand you can stay there overnight. Is that right?"

"A bed-and-breakfast. Yes. And there are vacancies right now, I believe."

"Well, that sounds perfect. I've just arrived from Oban and haven't made arrangements yet, so I'll check in at the castle. Thank you, young man. What's your name?"

"I'm David McCrimmon."

"Right, David. I'm Mike Marsh." The man offered his hand and David shook it. "Perhaps I'll see you at the castle," he concluded.

"Sure." David turned and started down the street. He still had twenty minutes to put in, and there was a bookshop on the next street. As he rounded the corner, he glanced back; Mike Marsh was still standing by the car, and he waved.

When David returned to the car, his arms full

of pink butcher's parcels, he saw that the envelope of pictures had fallen to the floor. After stowing the meat in the trunk, he picked up the envelope, fastened it with the button and string fastener, and returned it to the seat. It would be some time before he could share them with Sandy, and he didn't want to lose any.

* * *

The eleven o'clock tour was over and at Sandy's suggestion most of the tourists headed for the tearoom, recently opened in the castle basement. She waited to see that all were seated before finding a free table for herself in the corner.

David came over to her. At this time of day his duties required that he wear a tartan apron and take orders from the hungry tourists.

"Excuse me, madam," he said formally. "I regret I have to look after the paying customers first. In the meantime here's something for you to look at."

"Well, thank you sir. What's this? Ah. The pictures."

She had them spread out on the table before her when the visitors had all been served and David was able to join her.

He set down a teapot and a plate of scones in front of her.

"I anticipated your order," he said. "How did I do?"

"Perfectly, my good man," she said magnanimously. "I will double your tip."

"Why not triple it," suggested David with a grin. "Three times zilch is still zilch. Or better still, if you let me join you I will refund the entire amount."

"Well, that's generous of you. Please do."

"Just a minute then. I'll just go and get a sandwich."

He rejoined her a few minutes later. "What do you think of the pictures?"

"Beautiful photography. I must say you take great pictures."

"It's the camera," he said modestly. "Even I can't go wrong with it. But do you think they'll do any good? I mean — do you see anything that might help solve the mystery of Archie MacDonald's death?"

She shook her head slowly. "No. Well — I don't really know what I'm looking for." She gathered the pictures together to make room for her lunch. The one taken in the cave was on top. She tapped it with her finger. "You took two of these, didn't you? What happened to the other one? Didn't it turn out?"

"Yes. It should be there somewhere." He shuffled through the pictures, then shook his head. "That's odd. I must have dropped it in the cafe . . . oh, well, we've got one good one, anyway. Or I could have another of the missing picture developed from the negative, if you like."

"I don't suppose it matters." She sighed. "I

don't see anything in any of the pictures that's going to be any help. At least you have some good pictures of Hebridean scenery to take home with you. Too bad you didn't get one of that big bull seal that almost upset us."

"Yes, I wish I had. But I was too scared," admitted David. "It was so sudden I didn't have a chance. Unless — " He picked up the cave picture again, and looked at it carefully before shaking his head. "No such luck. I thought it might be there — just a shadow in the water. But it isn't."

"Perhaps in the other cave picture — the one you lost . . . ?"

"No. That one was aimed even higher than this one. It shows the shelf farther up."

"What? You mean there was a higher shelf than these?"

"Yes. Didn't you notice it? About four feet higher, I would say. With a seal on it too."

"No, David. I doubt very much if you saw a seal away up there."

"Why do you say that?"

She pointed to the picture again. "Those seals are there only because they were stranded when the tide went out. You can see the the high-water mark here, just above the shelf. The tide couldn't possibly have deposited anything higher than that. No — whatever you saw there, it wasn't a seal."

"So — what do you suppose it was?"

"I don't know. But it's intriguing. I'd like to find out."

"Well, that's easy enough," said David. "We'll take the negative in and have another copy made."

He tipped the envelope so the negatives slipped out onto the table. He held them up to the light, strip by strip, then shook his head, puzzled. "I can't find either shot taken in the cave. They should be side by side. . . ."

"Was it a twenty-four exposure film?" asked Sandy.

"Yes . . . "

"Then the one you're looking for must be among the missing. Look. You've only got twenty negatives there."

She was right. There were only five strips of four negatives each.

"Wouldn't you know it," muttered David. "One strip missing and it has to include the one picture I lost. Just my luck."

"Yes," said Sandy, frowning. "Quite a coincidence, wouldn't you think?"

He looked at her sharply. "Of course. What else could it be? We'll go to the photographer's tomorrow and complain. They might be able to find it. And we can go back to the cafe and see if anyone turned a picture in."

"Yes, we can do that." She was silent for a moment, drumming her fingers on the table.

"Your tea," said David, "is getting cold."

"Oh. Yes." She poured out a cupful and sipped it slowly. "You're sure you saw *something* on the shelf?"

"Positive. Something the colour and size of a seal. I just took it for granted . . . "

"That's interesting. We have a coincidence, and I'm always suspicious of coincidences. . . . Well, as you say, we can check in the cafe and the photographer's tomorrow — and have another look in the car in case they dropped out of the envelope." She finished her tea in one swallow and rose to her feet.

The man who was sitting at the table close behind Sandy took some money from his pocket. Leaving it on the table he stood up and approached.

"I enjoyed your tour, Miss — Sandy. This is a fascinating place. I have taken your advice and booked a bed-and-breakfast room. Perhaps you can suggest some other places of interest in the vicinity?"

"Certainly — and thank you, Mr. — ?"

"Turner. But since you invited us all to call you Sandy, you better call me Cliff. And your friend is — ?"

"I'm David. David McCrimmon."

"Pleased to meet you. Perhaps you'll be in the lounge this evening and can give me some suggestions?"

"Yes, we'll be there. Mrs. MacAllister serves tea and scones between nine and ten, and we try never to miss her scones."

Mr. Turner smiled briefly. "Right. Thank you both."

He turned and left the room. David looked after him, puzzled.

"Now where," he wondered, "have I seen that man before?"

"I doubt you have. He arrived at the castle just before the tour started. Unless you happened to run into him in town."

"Maybe . . . yes, that's it. He was in the cafe this morning when I stopped in for coffee. He came in and sat at the table next to me. I remember him because of his nose. Did you notice it?"

"His nose? Not particularly. It's not extra big or anything."

"No, but it's extra short. Which means he has an extra long upper lip."

"Oh? Yes, I suppose he has. I didn't take that much notice. I'll have to take a closer look when we meet him tonight. . . . "

7

The bed-and-breakfast guests gathered in the lounge that evening for a late snack before bed, as was the custom in Ramshaw Castle.

David looked around at the assembled people eating and drinking — just a few strangers from scattered corners of the world brought together by chance in this old castle that stood partially in ruins, partially restored, on the lonely moors of Lewis.

There were the Wades. They pronounced it "wide," which was appropriate, since they *were* wide. He was a roly-poly man composed of one round shape on top of another; like a baseball sitting neckless on top of a soccer ball, with spindly legs attached. He carried a pipe in his mouth, one that curved out of his mouth, swept down to rest on his chin, then curved up again to form a black bowl, presently empty. But apparently it could produce voluminous smoke, if his permanently squinting eyes were any indication. His wife was vast, spreading from small feet up and out in all directions, currently overflowing a large arm chair. Her pink cheeks almost obscured her bright eyes when she laughed — which was often.

They came from some corner of England where the natives played fast and loose with their aitches, dropping them from some words, then retrieving them and tacking them onto other words, where they had no business being. The Wades were " 'appy and hexcited to be 'ere."

David liked the Wades.

Then there were Marcel and Louise Cadeau from France. They taught English in their home country and their command of the language was almost flawless. Only the occasional accent on the last syllable of the word instead of the first gave them away. And Louise, too, had sporadic problems with her aitches. Mrs. MacAllister, who with good reason was proud of her scones, noticed that Louise's plate was empty and asked her, "And where are your scones, Madame Cadeau?"

"I hate them," responded Louise happily.

David, who had French-Canadian friends, recognized a potentially disastrous situation. "I ate mine too," he said quickly. "Could we have some more, Mrs. MacAllister?"

The cook beamed. "Of course."

The Cadeaus (or should that be Cadeaux,

David wondered) were both in their thirties, fresh faced and exuding good health, anxious to put on their hiking boots and tramp the wide-stretching moors.

David liked the Cadeaus.

Then there was the man from the tearoom, Cliff Turner. He was standing by the fireplace, elbow on the mantel. He was probably in his forties, David judged. There was a touch of frost at his temples and his forehead was expanding, though the hair, when you reached it, was thick and curly. He was wearing black-rimmed glasses to help in reading the tourist brochures displayed on the mantel. David couldn't help wondering what effect a moustache would have. Would it accentuate or diminish that unusually long upper lip?

And there was Mike Marsh, the bearded man who walked with a limp. He had been sitting back in a dimly-lit corner behind a newspaper, moving frequently as if in a futile effort to find comfort, apparently paying scant heed to those around him. But David noticed that now and then he folded down a corner of his paper and looked at each of the others present, appraisingly; and warily, it seemed, at Alec MacAllister.

For Alec was there too, waiting to take his wife home when her long day was over. He was dressed as David had last seen him, in a heavy sweater and thick pants tucked into sea boots. He probably dresses like that all the time, thought David. Except he likely takes his boots off to go to bed.

That was it, except for Sandy and David. She had exchanged her tour guide uniform for sneakers, jeans and a Fair Isle sweater. He remembered when he had first met her, a barefoot crew member on her uncle's trawler; then here on their first visit to the castle as guests of the Laird of Ramshaw, Sandy in a gown of French silk, with the lights of a hundred candles dancing in her eyes. And there was that night when she sat in the canoe and sang sad Gaelic songs while he paddled down the Moon Road. . . .

Cliff Turner put the brochures down and turned to Sandy.

"You were going to suggest places of interest to visit while I'm here, Sandy," he reminded her.

"Oh aye. Well, I suppose it depends on what interests you. What would that be now?"

"History, and castles. I've only been to Stornoway so far and the castle there has no history worth talking about. It can't be more than one hundred and fifty years old."

"Aye, that's right. I believe there's nothing left of the original MacLeod castle. And this is the only other castle on the Long Island that is more than a heap of stones. If you're interested in churches, there are two very old ones. The one at Rodel in Harris is four or five hundred years old, and there's an older one on the northern tip of Lewis. Then of course there are the Standing

Stones of Callanish."

"Oh yes," said Louise Cadeau enthusiastically. "You must see those. Why, the circle there is even better than Stonehenge. Not as elaborate, perhaps, but much more impressive — perhaps because of the loneliness. It is a fascinating place. One can imagine all sorts of ancient mysterious rituals taking place there." She shivered in pleasurable fear.

Her husband half smiled. "It probably has nothing to do with that sort of thing. Some people believe they were built for astronomical purposes. But I don't suppose we'll ever know for sure. They were erected thousands of years ago, were they not?"

"I believe so," nodded Sandy. "And there's something even older nearby. A broch dating from the Iron Age. An ancient fortress — *really* ancient . . ."

"Well, 'Enery and I didn't come here for 'istory," broke in Mrs. Wade. "We 'eard all about your wide hopen beaches on Lewis and that's what we come for."

"There are lots of those too." Sandy stood up and pointed out a spot on a large-scale wall map of the Hebrides. "Perhaps the closest would be on at Melbost." She turned back to the Wades. "You would have been nearer had you stayed in Stornoway."

"We meant to." Mrs. Wade nodded and her cheeks rippled like jelly. "But there were no vacancies. We set out looking for a b-and-b and this was the first one we come to. But it's not far back there. We'll drive over tomorrow if the weather's decent."

"Good idea," encouraged Sandy. "The predictions are for sun and warm temperatures. A perfect day to spend on the beach. Mrs. MacAllister will make up a lunch for you if you like."

Cliff Turner left the fireplace with a touch of impatience and sat in one of the easy chairs, removing his glasses and tapping them on his knee.

"To get back to castles. There's a small island somewhere in the Minch with an old castle on it. I forget the name. Do you know what I'm talking about?"

"Oh aye, you're likely thinking of Sgarbeg. That's the name of both the island and the castle. Perhaps you read about it in the papers. Sgarbeg has been in the news lately."

Cliff hesitated. "Yes, it seems to me . . . What was that all about anyway?"

"The man who rented the grazing lost his life in a storm. His boat was wrecked on the rocks."

"Oh yes, I remember. Still, I would like to see the ruins of the castle. Is there any transportation out to the island?"

"Perhaps," suggested David, "you and Mr. Marsh could get together. He's looking for a boat to hire — aren't you, Mr. Marsh?"

The bearded man looked startled. "Oh, no — I

mean, I doubt if we're interested in the same things." He shook his head and disappeared again behind his newspaper. "I certainly have no desire to visit *that* island."

"Oh!" David was rather taken aback. He turned to Cliff Turner again. "Then maybe Mr. MacAllister could help you."

The lobster man hesitated, then spoke in his slow and methodical way. "Oh aye, if it's transportation you're looking for and not luxury. My *Maisie* is available — for a price. But maybe it would be unwise to go to Sgarbeg. In fact I advise against it."

Cliff looked surprised. "Why, for heaven's sake?"

Again a pause, before Alec shook his head. "It has more than one name, yon island. Oh aye, it's Sgarbeg on the map, but there are others. . . . "

Sandy was puzzled. "You mentioned that before, Alec. What do you mean?"

"Perhaps you haven't heard, being from the west coast. And the name was almost forgotten, until Archie's accident. Now it's back. People are calling it Death Island again."

"Death Island!" Sandy was startled. "You mean to say Sgarbeg is *that* Death Island — of the plague and the curse?"

"Ah," said Alec significantly. "You *have* heard of it. Aye, that's the island, right enough."

"Wait a minute," said David eagerly. "What's this about a plague — and a curse?"

"A curse on the Island of Death," said Sandy, somberly. She looked around at the assembled guests. "I'll tell you about it. . . . "

8

"It was many years ago — don't ask me how many — when Death came to the island," Sandy began.

"Elspeth Campbell was the young and beautiful daughter of Campbell of Cladich. She was desperately in love with a nobleman, young Lord Lammond. But Cladich had other plans for his daughter. He was determined that she should marry the chief of the clan MacFarlane. You see, MacFarlane was an old man with no heirs, and was no longer likely to produce any. His widow would inherit all the lands of the MacFarlanes. Thus one more vast estate would pass without a fight into the grasping hands of the Campbells.

"But Elspeth refused point-blank to heed her father's wishes. In a rage he banished her from his lands to a lonely, forbidding castle on a lonely, forbidding island. And that island, of course, was Sgarbeg. It belonged to a MacLean who was kin to Cladich's dead wife. There Elspeth was to stay until she came to her senses and agreed to marry her father's choice.

"So she was locked away in a tiny, cold tower room, from which her only escape would be by the window — to be dashed to pieces on the rocks far below. Her only contact was her faithful servant, Auld Meg; and that contact was but the glimpse of a face, the touch of a hand through a barred grille high up on the iron-bound door, and a hurried word of encouragement when her meagre rations were handed in to her. Meg was under constant watch and had no opportunity to help Elspeth in any way.

"For many days young Lord Lammond had no idea what had happened to his lost love. He heard conflicting reports: that she had died, that she had spurned him and fled to where he would never find her. He refused to believe any of them. The Campbells were ancient enemies of the Lammonds, but that would not stop him. He went to Cladich, determined to face Elspeth's father and find out the truth.

"What he didn't know as he strode up to the castle gate was that the plague had swept Cladich. Everyone was infected, and many, including Cladich himself, were on the point of death.

"Lammond was amazed that no one challenged him. He was even more amazed when, unhindered, he swept into the presence of Cladich himself. In his excitement he failed to notice the shadow of death on Cladich's face and the putrid stench of the Black Death in the room.

" 'Sir,' he said, 'I have come to find out what happened to your daughter, and to claim her as my bride.'

"Whatever reaction Lammond expected, it could never have been what happened next. Cladich held out his arms, clasped the young man to his chest and kissed him. 'She is on Sgarbeg, and you may have her,' he said. Then, before Lammond could gather his scattered wits, the old man began to laugh wildly.

" 'You may have her, but she won't have you. I have the plague and I'm dying, and I have just passed the plague on to you. In a week you will be dead too.'

"For days young Lord Lammond wandered his estates, waiting for the sickness to strike. But it didn't. His health continued to be as good as ever. Days went by and he showed no sign of illness. So he concluded that Cladich's plan had failed. He had somehow escaped the dread disease. In high hopes he sailed for Sgarbeg.

"But as he stepped ashore nausea swept over him and he fell to the ground. Not only that — the Black Death had reached Sgarbeg ahead of him, and almost everyone on the island was infected. Only Elspeth, because of her isolation, had escaped; and for some unknown reason, so had Auld Meg.

"From her tower window Elspeth saw her

lover approaching. Her joy was unbounded —
until Meg told her the sad news that because of
his illness, Lammond refused to come to her.

" 'Then tell him I am already infected,' she
cried. 'Tell him I am sick unto death and want
only to see him and hold him in my arms before
I die.'

"At first Meg objected, but Elspeth cried, 'If
you love me, do as I bid.' So Meg brought Lammond to the tower room. She removed the keys
from a dying sentry and let the young lord in to
the prison.

"And so, the two lovers met, and rather than
wait for a slow and painful death they leapt from
the window high in the tower and were dashed
to pieces on the rocks far below.

"Weeks later an expedition from the mainland
came to Sgarbeg. They found everyone dead from
the plague — but one. Auld Meg was there, still
alive. But alone, surrounded by death, she had
gone mad. As they struggled to carry her away
she cried a curse on the island: that all who came
there would die before their time.

"And that," Sandy concluded, "is the legend of
Death Island."

There was a moment of silence — a moment
in which David shivered, remembering that wild
night on Sgarbeg when he heard the haunting
cry.

Then there was a burst of applause, which
Sandy acknowledged with a dramatic bow.

"Very well told," said Louise Cadeau admiringly. "I will *not* go anywhere near Death Island, you may be sure."

"But it's just a legend," Cliff pointed out drily.

"Aye, but a legend based on fact," said Alec slowly. "And when you think on the history of the island since, you wonder."

"Oh come!" Cliff was sceptical. "Because one person died accidently?"

"Och no, not just one. Archie is one of many. The island was abandoned for centuries and the castle fell into ruin. The MacLeans still owned it but they never went back to live there. They finally sold it to an Englishman who was going to use it for a summer home, but his wife died the first year unexpectedly and he's never been back. He rented out the grazing to Sandy Murchison but he died of cancer, and then it went to Archie, and you know what happened to him."

"And then — " Mike Marsh spoke up unexpectedly from his corner — "there was the shipwreck. What was her name? The *Neptune*."

Alec looked at Mike curiously, then nodded slowly. "That's right. She went down with all hands. And that's not all. There was the salvage crew."

"You don't mean to say that something happened to them, too," wondered Sandy.

"Not all of them. Just the two. The two that hired my *Maisie* to finish the job. They're both dead."

"What happened?"

"Accidents. One drowned, and the other was hit by a car. Hit-and-run. So you see," he turned to Cliff Turner, "there's reason enough why they are once again calling it Death Island."

"Perhaps you should steer clear of Death Island, Mr. Turner," suggested Marcel Cadeau.

"You're quite right," said Mrs. Wade. "You just come to the beach along of me and 'Enery and never mind them islands. What's another old castle anyway?"

"You may be right at that, Mrs. Wade." But Cliff wasn't looking her way. He was looking at Sandy and David, speculatively. "Perhaps we should *all* steer clear of Death Island."

9

"Well, that's that. Now what?" Sandy and David sat together on the wharf in Stornoway, their legs dangling over the side. Colourful fishing boats were tied up three and four deep in front of them. Beyond the latticework formed by their masts and spars the turrets of Lewis Castle peeked out from the trees.

"The photographer insists he gave us all the negatives," summarized David. "No one found a picture in the cafe. Neither the picture nor the negative was in the car. I've gone over what happened time and again. There's simply no way that picture and matching negative could have been lost accidentally. But that seems to leave only one alternative."

"Which is?"

"Someone deliberately stole them. And that doesn't make any sense at all."

"Maybe not to us," said Sandy seriously, "but it must make sense to the thief."

"Well — sure. But *we* have to know — why?"

"And how, and who? Lots of questions; to start with, how did anyone else know there was such a picture in the first place? Until we get back out there and have another look in the cave, we won't have any answers. You know, I have this . . . feeling that there's a connection here with the *Neptune*."

"How do you mean?"

"Well — suppose the divers found something on the wreck. Something valuable. They decided to keep it for themselves. They knocked Alec MacAllister out so he wouldn't interfere while they hid it in the cave."

"And it's still there two years later? That doesn't make sense."

"But remember both divers were killed, perhaps before they had a chance to move it. We should ask Alec when that happened."

David sighed. "It's all just guesswork. Maybe we're letting our imaginations run away with us. That's what the police would tell us, I'm sure, if we were foolish enough to say anything to them."

"Yes, and . . . " Sandy stopped, and caught his arm. "Speak of the devil! Here's one of them now."

He followed the direction of her gaze. A man was approaching, a squat, sandy-haired man, swinging along the wharf towards them.

He had already seen Sandy and David. He joined them with a welcoming smile. "Sandy

MacLeod. How's the Scourge of Ramshaw to-day?"

She laughed, flushing. "That's an awful name to give us," she objected. "Just because we were lucky enough to trap the Laird. . . . You haven't met David, have you. This is Sergeant Hummock. David McCrimmon."

"Pleased to meet you." He gripped David's hand briefly, and sat down beside Sandy. "Sent any more people to jail lately, Sandy?"

"No, 'fraid not," she said. "Sorry about that. Is there anything new yet — about Archie Macdonald's death?"

"New? No, why should there be? It was accidental, obviously." He looked at her keenly. "Or don't you agree?"

"Well, I just wondered," she said evasively. "I just can't imagine why Archie would go anywhere near the cliffs in that weather."

The policeman shrugged. "Other people have wondered that too. I don't suppose we'll ever know. Just one of life's little mysteries. People make mistakes, and it costs them."

"And you aren't making any effort to find out why?"

He grinned at her. "Maybe we are and maybe we aren't. That's police business. You found the body. You've done your part."

"Oh. I suppose we've been put in our place, Davie. By the way, Sergeant, Alec MacAllister was talking about the salvage crew who were cleaning up after the wreck on Sgarbeg two years ago. He said two of them died in accidents since then. Do you know anything about that?"

"Well, I think he's only partly right. One of them drowned, certainly. The other was badly hurt in a hit-and-run traffic accident — probably crippled for life. But he didn't actually die." He looked at her curiously. "What about it?"

"Do you know *when* the accidents happened? Soon after the wreck, or recently?"

"Well, as a matter of fact, both. I mean, one drowned in a salvaging accident a month or so after his job on Sgarbeg. The other was hurt several months ago. We weren't involved in either case — one man died in Oban harbour and the other was hit on the streets of Glasgow. But we were informed. Why do you ask? Is it this nonsense about 'Death Island' I've been hearing?"

"Yes," said Sandy eagerly, "that's it. Death Island. It is curious, don't you think? So many deaths connected with one place?"

He snorted derisively. "As I said, nonsense. It's stretching a point to say either one of those men had any connection with Sgarbeg. Don't you listen to superstition, Sandy. Sgarbeg is just another island." He stood up, brushing off the seat of his pants. "If you find any more bodies, give us a call. But don't look for mysteries where there aren't any. Nice to meet you, David. See you both around."

David watched him go. "Well, that didn't help any. He's probably right. We're looking for mysteries where there aren't any."

10

A brilliant moon bathed the castle in a soft warm radiance, smoothing the stones of the ancient walls, picking out the cars in the parking lot, casting deep shadows behind the towers and below the curtain walls.

David took a deep breath of the bracing air. "Sandy!" he called, softly.

"Yes? What is it?" She slipped out the door, pulling it to behind her. "Oh look at that moon! What a glorious night!"

"Yes, isn't it. How are you doing? All the guests tucked safely in their beds?"

"Well, they're on their way, anyway. You should see Mrs. Wade. She looks like a boiled lobster."

"Oh, she does, eh? Then I presume she found a beach all right?"

"Beach, wind and sun," Sandy confirmed. "It looks painful, but she's quite happy. Mr. Wade's

68

the same pasty colour as the day they arrived. He must have wrapped himself in a beach towel — or spent the day in the pub. And the Cadeaus have retired weary but happy after hiking up near the Butt all day."

"How about Cliff Turner?"

"He hasn't come in yet, but we don't have to wait for him. He has a key. We can't let a moon like that go to waste. Would you like to go for a walk?"

"I have a better idea. I've never seen the Standing Stones at Callanish by moonlight. How about driving out there?"

"Oh, good idea. Just a minute while I fetch a cardigan. Here are the keys. You can drive if you like."

David slipped in behind the wheel of the Nova. The car belonged to Sandy's uncle, but he was away and she had the use of it for the summer.

In a few minutes they were driving along the single-lane road. The countryside lay revealed all around in the moon's lustre. Whitewashed cottages scattered across the moors reflected the moonlight here and there, and the white shapes of the ever-present sheep moved like ghosts by the roadside.

At their destination they pulled off the road. David slid out from behind the wheel and joined Sandy in front of the car. The Standing Stones of Callanish stood out against the moonlit sky, straggling across the hilltop before them like a line of mourners in a funeral procession.

David shivered. "Eerie, isn't it."

Sandy moved close to him, her hand seeking his.

"Aye. You would expect to see ghosts here, wouldn't you?"

"Yes. Tell me about the stones, Sandy. I know no one knows the real reason why they were erected, but there must be lots of theories."

"Oh, aye, lots. The oldest is that they were once men who were turned to stone by a wicked sorcerer. No one knows why — or what the secret is to bring them back to life."

"Wouldn't that be a shock! To come back to life after thousands of years! Think of the changes they'd see."

"Not here, they wouldn't. Time stands still in the Hebridean countryside. Of course there are several theories to do with religion. You can't tell from here, but there is a pattern to the way they are laid out. Some think they represent the Celtic cross, but that's impossible. They were erected long before the birth of Christ."

"Druids, then?"

"That's more likely. The stones form avenues that lead to a central circle. There were probably religious rites held there. Sacrifices. Maybe even human sacrifices. More recently there were tales of ghosts flitting here and there among the stones. They turned out to be the invention of Big Nose Stronach."

"Who on earth is Big Nose Stronach?"

"The Lewis murderer. He hid out here between deeds. And staged ghosts to keep people away. They used to hear the most haunting sounds whenever they came close. He created those too, by blowing on a huge conch shell."

"I hope," said David, "that he won't be here tonight."

"Very unlikely, since he died more than a hundred years ago. Of course you never know about *his* ghost."

David laughed, not very convincingly.

"Let's take a closer look."

Hand in hand, with hushed footsteps, they entered a labyrinth of looming shapes and lurking shadows.

They started down a broad avenue formed by brooding monoliths, some small, others towering over their heads, their shadows carpeting the aisle before them. It seemed to David that as he and Sandy passed, they leaned a little closer and whispered menacingly to each other — and yet there was no wind. Their hands tightened and they walked a little closer together. In a few moments they stood at the hub, a wide circle ringed by thirteen stones. There was a dry-stone cairn in the centre, moon-splashed.

"That's where the sacrifices were made," said Sandy, low-voiced.

David nodded. He could almost see them, a ring of priests in long white robes, with hoods

71

shadowing their faces; one of the priests, stepping forward, raising a knife above his head, the blade winking in the moonlight . . . . He mentally shook himself to be rid of the fantasy.

"Marcel Cadeau was probably right. It had nothing to do with such things at all." David tightened his hand on Sandy's and pulled her closer. "It's too beautiful a night to think of sacrifices." He looked around at the silent, watchful pillars, and it seemed to him that something moved, a shadow maybe, near the entrance. "Beautiful, but eerie."

"Yes. It's lovely, Davie." She spoke softly. Her head was against his shoulder. He looked down at her. The moonglow highlighted her hair and when she looked up at him it was in her eyes, warm and intimate.

"Sandy," he whispered, "I've known you . . . " He hesitated, searching for words. "I wanted to tell you . . . "

She smiled at him. "This is no time for speeches, Davie. That moon doesn't want words, it wants action." She reached up and put her arms around his neck and pulled his face down to hers.

At that moment, out of the corner of his eye, he saw it: a stab of flame in the darkness. And he heard it: the sound of a shot shattering the silence, the slap of a bullet on the rock behind him, the whine of a ricochet.

For a moment they stood, clasped together,

frozen in shock.

Then they flung themselves on the ground, and he pulled her into the shelter of the nearest stone.

"Someone's *shooting* at us," he gasped, incredulously.

Her hand closed on his. It was shaking. "We've got to get out of here. Did you see where the shot came from?"

"Yes. Back near the entrance." He risked a quick look around the edge of their shelter. He could see no movement. He looked overhead. The moon that had been their friend was their enemy now, bathing the whole scene in a ghostly glow. "Blasted moon!"

Sandy was looking around desperately. "There are deep shadows over there. Bushes. A ditch. We'll have to make for that."

"Right. One stone at a time. And we'll split up. Two targets are harder to hit than one. You go straight back for a bit before turning. I'll go this way. Give me a step or two before you go."

"But — all right." It was no time to argue.

Another quick look, in time to see a shadow moving, flitting between the stones, coming closer. As long as he — she — whoever it was kept moving, he wasn't likely to shoot.

"Go!" whispered David. He darted across an open space to another shelter. Sandy was going too, dodging from one obelisk to the next. David watched her for a moment. Yes, that was the best bet. Keep moving. Take advantage of the shadows cast by the inscrutable columns.

It was a mad dash then, darting from one to the next — the odd glimpse of Sandy doing likewise — no time to look for their pursuer.

He came to the outer edge of the labyrinth. There was an open stretch to cross now, before he could reach the shadows. A quick reconnoitre. Then there was Sandy, running ahead of him, plainly visible in the moon's radiance. Well, as he had said, two targets were better than one. He was running too, bent double, dodging this way and that as he ran. And at last he flung himself into the welcome gloom. He was into a bush, with branches that clawed at him, scratching his face, then he was rolling down an embankment.

He lay at the bottom for a moment, gasping for breath. Where was Sandy? He had lost sight of her, but there had been no more shots. She must be all right.

"Davie!" There she was, bending over him. "Did you see anyone? Are they still after us?"

"I don't know. I saw someone once, just for a moment, dodging between the stones. What's going on? It must be a madman. Your Big Nose What's-His-Face come back to life. Ghosts don't shoot guns — do they?"

"No. I don't know. Let's take a look and see if anyone's still after us."

They climbed back up the bank and parted the branches. The stones stood in silence, as mysterious as they had been for thousands of years, untouched by time. There was no sign of life.

David shivered. "Where *is* he? Has he given up? Maybe he's a hermit living here and he just wanted to scare us away."

"If so, he succeeded," said Sandy grimly. "He didn't have to come *that* close to scare us off. I heard the bullet."

Yes, thought David, if Sandy hadn't pulled my face down to hers at just that precise moment . . .

"We'll have to skirt around to get back to the car. Keep in the shadows as much as possible. He may still be looking for us."

"There *aren't* any shadows." She was right. The treeless landscape lay wide open in the moon's unforgiving glow. "We'll stay right here for a while anyway. Be ready to run if we see him coming. He must know we're here. There's no where else to hide."

"If only I had a weapon of some kind. A club. Anything. Even a dead branch . . . "

A quick search in the darkness produced nothing other than thin branches that snapped in David's fingers.

"Okay," he said. "That's out. I hope you've been praying, Sandy. You've got us out of tight spots that way before now."

"Of course I have. Davie. Don't worry, we'll be all right. We can't get back to the car without — wait! Maybe we can."

"How?"

"The North Road can't be far away. It must be just beyond that hill. It's built up in places and runs through cuts here and there so there must be shadows of sorts. Maybe enough to get us back to the car. If not we can hide in a ditch until someone comes along. Someone's bound to, sooner or later."

Maybe not till morning, thought David. There wasn't much traffic through the night in this corner of Lewis, even at the height of the tourist season. But anything would be better than this.

"Right. One last check." There was still no sign of anyone. No movement. No sound.

"Okay. Let's go for it. Not too close together."

They ran across the open space, up a long rise, then they were descending and the black ribbon of road lay before them, stretching away to the right and left, deserted. There had been no hint of pursuit.

They stopped on the edge of the road and looked back. The brow of the hill hid their view of the enigmatic stones.

Sandy took a deep breath. "None of this makes sense," she complained. "Why would someone take a shot at us?"

"Hanged if I know. But no one came after us. It must have been a random act. Some punk out shooting for a lark. If he really meant to kill us he would have come after us."

"Either that," said Sandy, slowly, "or he'll go

back to our car and wait for us there."

"Uh-oh! I never thought of that. I'm glad you did. We might have walked into a trap. So we should go the other way and look for a telephone so we can call the police."

She shook her head. "I don't think there's a telephone for miles. There's — wait." They suddenly heard the sound of a car approaching from the direction of the Callanish gate. Then they saw the lights, sweeping across the moors as it negotiated a curve. For a moment they watched its approach, hesitating.

"It might be him," whispered Sandy. "Looking for us."

"Maybe," muttered David. "We'd better not take a chance. This ditch isn't very deep. We'll have to lie flat. And cover your face so the lights don't catch it. See, he's coming pretty slowly, as if he's looking for someone. I don't like the look of it."

The car was barely crawling along. Once it stopped, then came on again, as if it was sniffing out its prey, first along one shoulder, then the other.

Sandy and David crouched in the meagre ditch, ready to fling themselves flat. Then the car stopped. A beam of light shot out from the car roof, and raked across the hillside.

"Holy smoke!" David sprang up. "He's got a spotlight. He'll see us for sure. We'll have to run for it. Where the car can't follow."

"No! Wait!" She grabbed him. "It's all right, Davie. It's a police car!"

"The police! Well, thank God for that." Relief flooded over him.

They stood up, shakily, and started walking, hand in hand, down the road toward safety.

The spotlight had been extinguished and the car was coming on again, slowly. Then, apparently, they were seen. The car stopped at the rim of the road, the door opened and a man emerged and began to walk towards them, black in the glare of the headlights.

"Well, well. If it isn't the Scourge of Ramshaw again!"

"Sergeant Hummock!" cried Sandy. "Are we ever glad to see you."

"It's nice to be appreciated." He stopped then, and waited for them to join him. "What are you two doing out here?"

"Walking," said David, almost lightheaded in relief. "And, of course, dodging bullets."

"Now *that's* the part I'm interested in," said Sergeant Hummock. "Someone reported a gunshot. I didn't take it seriously, but thought I'd better check it out. Of course, I didn't know you two were anywhere nearby. You'd better give me the whole story."

They did so. The policeman listened without comment. "All right," he said, when they had finished. "Is that your car back there? The blue Nova?"

"Yes."

"Fine. Get in and I'll take you back. We'll cordon off the area and give it a thorough search in the morning. But first, perhaps you wouldn't mind showing me just where you were standing when the shot was fired?"

"We'll be glad to," said David. "And I must say you're very efficient. How did you get here so quickly?"

"Oh, that was luck. I was in the neighbourhood checking on a barking dog. Mrs. MacRae — you know her, Sandy — she lives across the bay at Linshader. Her dog was cutting up rough and she was afraid of prowlers. I couldn't find anything and was on my way back when an unidentified caller reported a gun shot in this area.

"I stopped one car. It was someone you know. Cliff Turner, who is staying at the Castle. Is that right? He was coming back from Barvas and drove right past here but he hadn't seen or heard anything. I expect it was some young fool who had a bit too much to drink. If so the sound of his own gun going off probably sobered him up in a hurry and he's long gone."

The police car pulled up beside Sandy's.

"I've called for assistance, and we'll put a guard on the site for the night and give it a good going-over in the morning. Now, Sandy and David, if you will just show me where you were standing . . ."

It was different, this time. In the presence of

the policeman the grim silent columns seemed to have lost their mystery. They reached the circle of thirteen stones.

"We were right here," said David, just a little self-consciously. "We were — pretty close together . . . "

"Like this," said Sandy. She put her arms around David's neck and spoke to the sergeant over her shoulder. "I was just about to kiss David when I heard the bullet. It hit the stone just behind David's head, right about there."

"Terrible timing," said the policeman sympathetically. "Let's see." He took a flashlight from his pocket and played the beam over the stone. "Yes, I believe you're right. There's a chip out of the stone. It must have ricocheted, too. And I would guess the shot came from . . . " He turned and looked back the way they had come. "From back there."

"That's right," confirmed David. "I saw the flash."

"Good. Well, the moon's bright, but not bright enough. There's not much we can do till morning. You two can go now. I know where to reach you if I need you."

He walked them back to their car. "I'll be waiting here till help arrives," he said, "so off you go. And — " he leaned in the window as Sandy inserted the key into the ignition, "just one other thing."

"Yes? What's that?"

"About Sgarbeg."

"Sgarbeg?" Sandy was startled.

"Not that I think this has anything to do with the island," said the sergeant quickly. "It's just that I know you, Sandy. And if there's anything going on out there that's not quite — legitimate, it's up to us to find out what. That's what we're paid for, you know."

"Oh! Yes. Of course. Yes, anything you say. Goodnight, Sergeant."

For a moment, as they drew away, neither spoke. Then Sandy broke the silence.

"He shouldn't have said that," she muttered. "I hadn't connected it at all. But I'll just bet he's right. There *is* a connection. Someone would rather kill us than have us go back out there — to Death Island." She looked challengingly at David. "I suppose you'll say my imagination is running away with me again."

But David shook his head. "No. As a matter of fact I've had the same thought myself. And I find myself wondering about our friend, Cliff Turner."

11

"Cliff Turner?" Sandy looked at David with interest. "What about him, Davie?"

"Well," said David, thoughtfully, "if someone stole that picture and negative, it *must* have been Cliff Turner. He was in the cafe when I was looking at the pictures, so he knew I had them, and no one else could have. He seems to be interested in Sgarbeg, doesn't he? He even said he wants to go out there. Did you notice, Sandy, that when he mentioned Sgarbeg Island last night he was looking at you and me — as if he was watching to see how we would react? And besides that he was in the vicinity of Callanish tonight. Coincidences? Maybe. Maybe not."

Sandy nodded slowly. "And there's someone else *I'm* wondering about. Mike Marsh."

"Mike Marsh? Why?"

"Remember what Sergeant Hummock said? He said that the salvage diver who was hurt in the traffic accident didn't die — but that he must be crippled. And just when strange things start happening at Sgarbeg a man with a bad limp shows up. And he wants to hire a boat."

"I hadn't thought of that. Actually, he could have ripped off the pictures, too — he was standing right by the car and could have seen them on the seat. But no — there's no way he could have known about them. Cliff Turner is our man, I think — though we might want to keep an eye on Mike Marsh."

"I think so. But we've hardly enough to make an accusation in either case," sighed Sandy. "Or even convince anyone else. What do you think really happened tonight, Davie? Is Sergeant Hummock right? Was it some drunk who didn't know what he was doing?"

"No, it wasn't," said David decisively. "Somo-one tried to kill us tonight, Sandy. Or at least to give us a bad scare. And if *that* was his objective, he succeeded very well. I got a glimpse of him. He was coming after us. No doubt about that."

"Then what happened? Why did he give up?"

"The only thing I can think of is that he saw or heard the police car coming, and ran."

"But how — but no one knew we were going to Callanish. D'you think someone followed us? We didn't see anyone."

"It could be. We weren't looking for anything like that. All I could see was the moonlight — and you."

Her free hand crept into his. "What are we going to do, Davie? If someone tried to kill us — will he try again?"

"I don't know. If we only knew *why*, we'd have a chance of answering that. But it's got to be connected with Sgarbeg Island, doesn't it? What else could it be?"

"D'you think Sergeant Hummock is right when he says we should forget it and leave it up to the police?"

"Yes, I think he's right. Except for one thing. They don't seem to be in any hurry to do anything, and until the matter's finished with, I have a feeling our lives are going to be in danger. Unless we can convince everyone that we *have* given up, whoever tried to kill us once will try again."

"We could put an ad in the paper," said Sandy whimsically. " 'Attention, all crooks. We the undersigned hereby relinquish all interest in Sgarbeg Island. Please just leave us alone.' How's that?"

She laughed, and halfway the laugh turned into a sob.

"Pull over for a minute, Sandy," he said.

She didn't argue. She steered to the edge of the road, and shut off the ignition, then turned to him. He reached out and pulled her into his arms, saying nothing, just holding her tightly and letting her cry.

He didn't know how many minutes passed

before she pushed herself back and looked up. "I'm sorry, Davie," she whispered. "I don't like being shot at. It scares me."

He gently brushed tears from her cheek. "Don't apologize. I think I needed that as much as you did. I was terrified — my knees still feel like rubber. I don't like this any more than you do. That's why we have to decide what we're going to do."

"Right." She sat up, still holding his hand. "We can't advertise, so even if we give up on Sgarbeg right now, this very minute, there's no way whoever is out there is going to know. I don't want to keep looking over my shoulder and living in fear. Davie, I'm sorry. Me and my curiosity got you into this mess."

"Forget that, Sandy. I could have backed out if I wanted to. Just keep saying your prayers."

"I will. And thank you, Davie." At his quizzical look she added, "Most people would laugh at me for praying. You never do."

"I've seen the results."

"Which most people would put down to coincidence."

"Not me," said David. "I've done it myself. I guess a lot of people do when they're in tight spots. I was praying tonight when I was dodging around those stones. Though I felt guilty about it."

"Guilty? Why?"

"Because — how can I ask God to come to my

rescue when I only call on him when I'm in trouble?"

She laughed softly. "There's one way to remedy that. Don't ignore him the rest of the time." She moved back behind the wheel, switched on the ignition and moved the car back onto the road. "So, what do you think we should do, Davie?"

"You said you don't like living in fear. Neither do I. I think the only thing to do is settle this thing once and for all. Go back out to Sgarbeg Island and find out what's going on."

She looked at him sideways. "The police won't like that," she reminded him.

"Maybe not, but no one's shooting guns at them. What do you think?"

"Oh, I agree. We have to go back. We have to go into the cave and see what's there."

"And how are we going to do that? Hire a boat again? I'm broke."

"No, we'll take Alec's lobster boat, the *Maisie*."

"*Take* it? Just like that?"

"Oh, I'll think up some excuse. Mrs. MacDonald will remember something else Archie left behind and we'll go back and look for it."

"Alec might not want to go."

"I hope not. He'll let us take the *Maisie*. There's no trick to handling her in calm weather. And it will have to be calm if we're to go into the cave. We'll be careful. The open sea isn't like the Standing Stones of Callanish. No one is going to sneak up on us out there without us knowing it.

86

What do you think?"

"I'm all for it. And as soon as possible. . . . "

A few minutes later they pulled into the parking lot below the castle. David indicated a car at the end of the line.

"Isn't that Cliff Turner's car?"

"Aye, I think so. He's back." She looked down the line of parked cars. "But Mike Marsh isn't. So *he* could have been at Callanish tonight too."

They entered the castle. They were in the servants' quarters here. They paused briefly before parting to go to their respective rooms.

"Good night, Davie. See you in the morning. Be sure to lock your door."

"You too." He reached forward and gave her a quick kiss on the forehead. "Good night, Sandy. When this is all over we'll start in where we left off when we were interrupted by a gunshot. But next time it won't be in an overgrown graveyard."

12

"Why, Sandy MacLeod! How nice to see you." A pleased smile lit up Jemmie Macdonald's face. "And your young man. Please forgive me. I forget your name."

"I'm David McCrimmon, Mrs. MacDonald. I mean Jemmie. *Ciamar a tha?*"

"Oh, *tha ga math*, laddie. And I thought you were Canadian!"

David grinned. "I am. But Sandy's been teaching me a little Gaelic."

"Well, good for you. Then maybe you'll know what I mean when I invite you in for a *strupak*?"

"Oh yes, I know that one. A cup of tea and maybe some oatcakes or shortbread."

"Right you are. Come away ben while I put the kettle on the fire." The wee woman ushered them into a tiny hall. "The parlour!" she decided. "We'll have a cup of tea in the parlour."

"Oh, please don't go to any trouble, Jemmie.

We'll be quite at home in the kitchen, you know."

"Oh aye, I ken that fine. But the minister left just a wee while ago and I have a fire going in the grate, so we'll go in there. Just you two have a chair while I see to a bite."

Like everything else about the house and its keeper the parlour was small and neat, and scrupulously clean. It was obviously used only on special occasions. The furniture was a little too hard for comfort, but it was cozy with the warmth of friendship. Prints of Highland scenery decorated the bright walls, and even the severe countenances of two elderly people peering from a picture on the mantel failed to dampen the cheerfulness of the atmosphere.

Jemmie MacDonald bustled in a few minutes later with a teapot in a cozy and a plate of oatcakes and cheese.

"There now, help yourselves. It's so good of you young folks to visit an old body like me."

"Och away, Jemmie!" protested Sandy. "You're not old."

"Aye, well, a body is as old as she feels, which makes me about ninety these days."

"Nonsense. You don't look a day over forty. How are you getting along on your own?"

Jemmie sighed. "When you've lived with someone for thirty years, then he's suddenly no longer there, it's — it's not easy. But they were good years. There are so many good memories."
Tears shone in her eyes for a moment. She

blinked them fiercely away. "But never mind me. How are things going at the castle?"

"Oh, that's a lot of fun. We have tourists from all over the world."

"Is that so! Fancy that! You must be asked many interesting questions."

"Yes, we are. Of course with an old castle like Ramshaw, history is the main interest. Anything I can say about the ghost or Bonnie Prince Charlie is sure to get a good response."

"And you, David? What do you do?"

"Oh — just about anything. I guess you would say I'm a handyman. Gardener, waiter, washroom attendant — wherever I'm needed. I'm having a great summer."

Mrs. MacDonald poured out the tea and passed the cream and sugar. "It was very good of you to go out to Sgarbeg to bring Archie's things back. That's some of his peat on the fire there now."

"That was no problem," Sandy assured her. "Are you certain there isn't anything else out there of his that we might have missed?"

"Oh, I don't think so. Not that I know of. And you said you had a good look around and didn't see anything more. Isn't that right?"

"Yes, that's right." Sandy hesitated. She took a sip of tea, then set her cup down. "Jemmie, we want your help."

"My help?" The wee woman was mystified. "Of course. But how can I help you?"

"Well, it's this way. We — David and I — think there's something . . . something strange about Archie's death." She looked enquiringly at the widow. Mrs. MacDonald frowned, and nodded slowly. "And that there's something going on out there on Sgarbeg that — well, that shouldn't be going on."

"Yes. There *was* something wrong. Why was Archie — where you found him? I have heard many a 'simple explanation,' and none that satisfies me. I don't think there are any answers — except one. You know the legend. Sgarbeg is the Island of Death."

"There must be more to it than that. Was there ever anything else? I mean, did Archie ever say anything to suggest there may be something going on there?"

Jemmie hesitated, then shook her head. "No, not really. I do remember once when I was there with him and we had to stay over because of a storm. We were watching the waterspout and I asked him what caused it. He told me about the cave, then he said, 'But there's more to it than meets the eye. There must be. Or why would those people . . . ' That's all he said. Something happened to distract us — I forget what. I remembered what he said afterwards but I was alone by then and I couldn't ask him to explain. After that it just slipped my mind. Until now."

"Could it be," suggested David, "that he saw

some people going into the cave that caused the waterspout?"

"Well, yes, I suppose that's possible."

Sandy leaned forward. "We think it's more than possible. The day we went out with Alec to bring back the sheep, David and I went into that cave. We didn't see anything unusual, but David took some pictures, and then one of the pictures was stolen before I had a chance to see it. Why? Was someone afraid there was something in the picture that I would recognize as being — out of place? Then last night we went out to Callanish, and someone shot at us — "

"Shot at you!" Jemmie was horrified. "My dear! That — that's terrible! Do you think it had something to do with Sgarbeg?"

"We think so. The police don't agree. They claim it was some drunk who didn't know what he was doing. But at the same time they advise us to steer clear of Sgarbeg."

"And so you should. Sandy — and David — listen to me. Nothing will bring Archie back. There may be something wrong going on but it's not worth you two risking your necks over. Leave it! Let the police handle it."

"But they aren't handling it. They don't think there's anything wrong. Look, Jemmie. We want to go back to Sgarbeg. Just the two of us. In broad daylight. We'll be safe enough. You can see for miles in all directions. No one will be hiding behind stones taking pot shots at us. We just want to take one more look in that cave, then we'll come back."

Mrs. MacDonald was worried. "I suppose . . . But I wish you would just leave it be."

"No," said Sandy decisively. "We can't do that. Our problem is a boat. We think Alec would let us take the *Maisie* if we had a good reason for going. That's why we hoped you might help. If you could think of something of Archie's that was lost, perhaps, and you can't find it anywhere, and you think it might be out there on Sgarbeg somewhere, and want us to go and look for it . . . "

She smiled. "Invent something, you mean. No, but if you're determined to go, I may have a better idea. Archie's father was a fisherman. Did you know? He owned a lugger and fished in the Minch, longline fishing. One day when he was out in stormy weather he was washed overboard and lost. That's why Archie hates the sea. He was just a lad when it happened, and saw his father go. The crew brought the lugger back and Archie left the fishing then and there. When the time came for him to make a living he took up sheep farming. The lugger was tied up at its old wharf down near the mouth of Loch Odhairn and left to rot. Archie didn't want to have any more to do with it."

"Couldn't he have sold it?"

"He never tried. He just wanted to forget it ever existed. Even when he took the grazing on Sgarbeg and he needed a boat to get back and forth he never considered the old lugger. Of course with the sails and all it was too much for one man to handle, but it was out of the question anyway."

"So you mean it's still down there at Loch Odhairn — probably rotting."

"Aye, it's down there, but it's not rotting. Our nephew from London asked Archie if he could have her and fix her up and Archie said yes, he was welcome to do whatever he liked with her. So Willie — that's our nephew — put a motor in her and took her out to sea two or three times when he was up on holiday. But then he lost interest in her and she's been there since, for two years or more. At least I suppose she is. Unless she's been storm-damaged, or sprang a leak for some reason. She *could* be sitting on the bottom, but I doubt it. I haven't laid eyes on her myself for ages. Anyway, the point is, if you're looking for some way out to Sgarbeg by yourselves without bothering anyone you're welcome to use the old lugger. What do you think?"

"Oh yes! It would be just what we want, if she's seaworthy." Sandy looked at David. There was eager excitement in her eyes. "What do you think, Davie?"

He grinned. "You're the sailor. Let's go and take a look anyway."

"Aye, do that," nodded Jemmie. "If you can't use her we'll think of something else, but she should get you to Sgarbeg and back. Oh yes, you'll need the battery to start the engine. It's out in the shed. And you will probably have to have it recharged."

"Wonderful. We'll run down this afternoon and look her over."

* * *

Half an hour, several cups of tea and numerous oatcakes later Sandy and David took their leave. In the hall Jemmie caught David's arm. "David, just a minute. Can I give you some advice?"

Mystified, David nodded, and bent his head down to hers. She whispered into his ear. A slow smile spread over his face.

"Thanks, Jemmie," he said. "I won't forget."

Sandy watched them suspiciously. As they departed, waving, she said, "What was that all about?"

"Oh, nothing much," said David evasively. "A secret. I'll tell you someday. When the time is appropriate." And she couldn't get any more out of him.

13

As it turned out, the lugger *was* on the bottom, but perhaps that was only because the tide was out. She looked like a beached whale, leaning drunkenly against the wharf, her keel lying in a pool of water left by the receding tide.

David stared at the boat from the car with a sinking heart.

"Holy smoke!" he muttered. "We hope to go to Sgarbeg on *that*?"

It was not an encouraging sight. She was old and cumbersome-looking, her heavy-timbered flanks scarred and battered. Flaking black paint clung here and there. Her single forward mast leaned to starboard even more than her uneven keel warranted and the spar that once held up the lugsail was long gone. There were holes visible in her tilted deck, and the tall wheelhouse slightly abaft of midships was made of warped, unpainted plywood.

For a moment Sandy made no reply, then she said brightly, "What did you expect? Another *Kittiwake*? She *is* a lugger, after all. Let's take a closer look."

They left the car and walked towards the boat, down to the shoreline rather than along the jetty that stood thin-legged out of the wet sand. They walked around the stern of the heavy hulk, noting the single propeller and the rudder. There was a crack the length of the rudder, but that apparently didn't worry Sandy so David shrugged it off. The exposed flank on the seaward side was substantial-looking in an ugly way. They approached the bow. Suddenly Sandy started to laugh.

"Look at that." She was pointing to the boat's name, painted in once-white letters on the black hull.

David tried to read it, and failed. "What is it? What's so funny?"

"There are a few letters missing," grinned Sandy, "but it's obviously supposed to be *Ealachan Ban*. Which, translated, is *White Swan*. Did you ever see anything that looked less like a white swan?"

"Somebody," grunted David, "has a warped sense of humour." He looked up to where, in his limited knowledge of ships, he figured the hawseholes should be. "Doesn't she have an anchor?"

"Probably not. We won't need one. We'll tie up at the wharf on Sgarbeg."

"Oh yes, that's another thing. How are we going to get into the cave? This boat, if you'll pardon the expression, will never fit through the opening."

"No," agreed Sandy. "We'll have to take something smaller along. How about one of those inflatable life rafts? I know where I can get one. They inflate automatically."

"Oh yes, I know what you mean. They don't come with outboards, do they?"

She laughed. "No, they come with paddles. So we paddle from the wharf to the cave. I wouldn't want to anchor this boat off the cave mouth anyway. We might attract attention, and that's something we don't want to do."

"If we get this thing going," said David, "we'll attract lots of attention anyway. Someone will board us to see if we have any animals in the hold, two by two."

Sandy giggled. She tucked her arm through David's. "Come on, Davie, this is going to be fun. Let's go aboard and make sure everything is working."

"Okay." David spoke like a martyr. "We might as well take the battery with us."

They went out along the jetty and left the battery on the end boards, then stepped onto the sloping deck. There was a large open space that had presumeably, at one time, had a removeable cover. David peered into it. It was dark below, except for a patch of reflected light. He looked at

Sandy in alarm. "There's water down there."

She took a look. "Aye, but not much. Probably just rain accumulated over the years. It's not a leak, if that's what worrying you. I'm going to test the wheel. Away you and look over the stern and see if the rudder answers to the helm."

"Aye aye, Captain. Holler when you're turning in case it's become disconnected."

She didn't have to holler. When he looked down from the deck the rudder, crack and all, was moving in response to her efforts.

"Okay, it's working." He returned to the wheelhouse. There was barely room for more than one inside, so he didn't try to squeeze in. "What else have you got besides the wheel?"

"Not much," she admitted. "This is what you call basic transportation. No options. There's a compass. An old one. Probably the one Noah used. But it seems to be working."

"We won't need one anyway," David pointed out. "We'll be sailing in good weather on a clear day. We'll just head straight for Sgarbeg. You can see it from here."

"Aye, that's right. There's the engine controls, and that's it."

"No radio?"

"No radio. Oh, there's this." She reached up and turned something over her head. A sudden banshee howl shattered the calm of the afternoon. David jumped a foot. Gulls rocketed from the water, screeching in protest.

"What — " gasped David, when he returned to the deck. "What was *that*?"

"Foghorn," said Sandy laconically.

"*Foghorn*? I bet half the people in Stornoway are diving for shelter right this minute. Thank God we won't need that either."

Sandy came out of the wheelhouse. "Let's get the battery in place and make sure the engine works."

There was a raised trap door behind the wheelhouse. They opened it up and were looking at the engine.

"That," David pointed out, "is where the battery goes. We'll have to attach the cables."

"There are spanners in the boot," said Sandy.

Rightly interpreting this as meaning there were wrenches in the trunk of the car, David nodded. "I'll be right back."

They had the battery in place in a few minutes.

"Now," said David, "let's check the gas. I mean the petrol. I hope no water got into it over the years."

"I don't see why it should," said Sandy. "We'll put in what we brought anyway and see what happens."

David went to the car for the petrol can. Sandy didn't wait for him. She returned to the wheelhouse and pressed the starter. The engine groaned and clanked and coughed alarmingly. Then it caught. A few moments of hesitant sputtering, then it was running relatively smoothly.

"I'm going to put it in gear," she called. "Check and see if the screw's turning."

David leaned far over the rail to see below the counter and in behind the rudder, where the propeller was clear of the sand.

"Okay," he shouted, suddenly elated. "It's turning. We're in business."

She stopped the engine and emerged from the wheelhouse.

"There's no petrol gauge, so we'll have to fill the tank and bring extra. I don't suppose we'll get too many miles to the gallon. And we'll bring a lunch and make a day of it. Anything else we should bring?"

David looked around at the tilting deck, the drunken mast and the wretched wheelhouse, then out over the gray waters of the Minch.

"Life jackets," he decided. "We need life jackets."

"All right," she conceded. "We'll take some. We won't need them but we'll take some. The *Ealachan Ban* may not be much to look at but she's a good ship. I can feel it."

"Well, if you can feel it, we've got nothing to worry about. You're the captain. I'm here to obey orders."

"All right then. March!"

Laughing, he saluted. Sandy's eyes suddenly widened, focussing on something beyond him.

"Don't look now," she whispered, "but we're being watched."

"I'm not surprised. That foghorn could have attracted half the population of Lewis." He waited a moment, then turned to follow her gaze.

There was a man standing on the crest of the hill beyond, looking at them. David waved. The intruder seemed to hesitate, then waved in return. For another moment he stood there, then turned and walked away, disappearing behind the hill.

"Did he seem familiar to you, Davie?" Sandy asked.

"Familiar?" He looked at her curiously. "No, not to me. He was too far away. But then I don't know anyone around here anyway except the people in the castle. Perhaps it was one of your local friends."

"Aye, likely you're right. Davie, are you coming to the late snack in the lounge tonight? I haven't seen Cliff Turner or Mike Marsh since we were shot at and they might be there tonight. I just wonder if they'll say anything . . . interesting."

"Yes, I'll be there."

* * *

Cliff Turner was there. So was Mike Marsh, once again in his chair in the shadows, saying little. The Wades and the Cadeaus too were all awaiting Mrs. MacAllister and her evening snack. They were apparently engaged in small talk, which ceased abruptly when Sandy and David entered.

"Here they are," cried Mrs. Wade. Her eyes were like buttons embedded in a pink cushion. "You poor kids. Imagine being shot at. It must have been 'orrible."

"Oh, you heard about that, did you?"

"Oh yes," said Marcel Cadeau. "Everyone knows about it, but not first-hand. Now we can hear all about it from the horse's bit."

"The horse's mouth," corrected Cliff Turner absently. "Yes, sit down and tell us what happened."

"I understand from Sergeant Hummock," said David, looking at Mr. Turner, "that you were near Callanish last night."

"Yes I was, as a matter of fact." Cliff sat down in a nearby chair and slung one leg over the arm. "I was coming back from Barvas — the long way, but it was a beautiful night for a drive. I saw the police car at the entrance into the circle and wondered what was going on. Then the sergeant came along and said there'd been a shooting. I had no idea you two were involved. What happened?"

"We don't really know," said Sandy. She looked directly at Mike Marsh. "You were out last night too, Mr. Marsh. Were you anywhere near Callanish?

"No. I was in Stornoway."

"Were you able to hire a boat?"

"Yes thank you."

Abrupt. Eager to avoid drawing attention to

himself. At least, that's how it seemed to David.

"But what *happened*?" demanded Mrs. Wade impatiently.

"We went to look at the stones in the moonlight and somebody shot a gun at us. That's all, really. We ran for it, and luckily for us the police car came along."

"Yes, you were lucky all right." Cliff Turner lit a cigarette and blew a smoke ring towards the ceiling. "Have they made any arrests yet, do you know?"

"I don't know. We haven't anything more from the police."

"That's not our fault." Sergeant Hummock had slipped into the room. He paused in the doorway, his eyes sweeping over the people assembled there. They paused when they came to Mike Marsh. A moment's hesitation, a fractional lifting of the brows in surprise, before passing on quickly — he recognized him, thought David. Interesting . . .

The policeman turned to Sandy. "We've been trying to reach you since noon. You've been out?"

"Yes, we called on Jemmie MacDonald. Why? Have you any more information?"

"No, not yet. We have a couple of leads and it shouldn't be too long before we get some results. I just wondered . . . " He paused. Mike Marsh had stood up.

"Excuse me," he said. "But I must make a phone call."

"If it can wait a few more minutes," suggested Sandy, "Mrs. McAllistair will be in with tea and scones any minute now."

Mike glanced at his wristwatch and shook his head. "Thank you," he said. "If I can I'll be back before you've finished."

He limped quickly across the room. It seemed to David that he deliberately avoided looking at the policeman, who had to step aside to let him out. When he was gone Sergeant Hummock resumed.

"I just wondered, now that you've had some time to recover from the shock, if you can recall anything else that might help us."

David and Sandy looked at each other, then shook their heads slowly.

"I don't think so," said David. "I did catch a glimpse of him just once. Did I tell you that?"

"No you didn't. Was that after the two of you split up?"

David hesitated. "No, I think — just before."

"And what did you see? I suppose it was too dark for you to give me a description."

"Oh yes. He was just a — a shadow."

"Tall? Fat? Anything at all?"

"No. He wasn't tall. About average. But then he might have been crouching. Really I'm afraid I can't help you at all."

The policeman sighed. "Oh well, never mind."

"I suppose," said Cliff Turner, "that it was just a random kind of thing. A drunk, maybe?"

"There's not much doubt about that. I hardly think Sandy and David could have enemies that might want to murder them."

"But that's terrible," Louise Cadeau's face was pale. "Out here? In the countryside? On the Island of Lewis? In London or Glasgow that kind of thing might happen, but surely not here? Why, Marcel and I were out there. We walked through the stones. Someone might have shot at us!" She caught her husband's hand. "We won't feel safe now, anywhere."

"Oh please," said Sandy. "Don't feel that way. It was just a one-in-a-million thing. Nothing like this will happen again for a hundred years."

"Maybe you're right," said Louise doubtfully. "But I *won't* feel safe. We were going to go hiking in Harris tomorrow, but now . . ."

"You go right ahead, Ma'am," said the policeman. "This was a local thing. We have our eye on a suspect. He's never gone this far before — he never had a gun before — but he's a troublemaker. If we can nail him this time it will put him out of commission for a long time. Now if you'll excuse me, I have work to do."

"So long, Sergeant. I hope you get him." Cliff Turner pinched the end of his cigarette. "Sorry. I should have asked permission before lighting up. I forgot. Mrs. Wade doesn't like smoke."

"No I don't," said that lady briefly. "Not cigarette smoke. Ah, here's Mrs. MacAllister with our tea." She contemplated a pile of hot buttered scones with happy anticipation.

* * *

Sandy slipped into David's room, closing the door behind her.

"Well?" she asked. "Did you notice anything?"

"Notice anything? What do you mean?"

"About what Cliff Turner said. He lied about coming back from Barvas."

"How do you know?"

"Because he would have come along that road we ended up on after the shooting, and we would have heard his car and seen the lights — or at least their glow. He must have come from the other direction. So why did he lie?"

David nodded slowly. "And another thing. He said, before Sergeant Hummock came in, that he saw the police car and stopped. That's not what the sergeant said. Remember? The way he told it, it was the other way around. Not that it matters one way or the other, but our friend Cliff Turner slipped up."

"Do you think he — he could be the one that shot at us?"

"I guess he *could* be. But what about Mike Marsh? Did you notice how Sergeant Hummock reacted when he saw Mike? I'm sure he recognized him — maybe he *is* the diver who was injured in that traffic accident. If he's come back for something on Sgarbeg, he'd want to get there before anyone else started poking around. . . ."

David was silent for a while. "When can we sail in the *White Swan*, Sandy?"

"Just as soon as possible," said Sandy with determination. "The very first day we have seas calm enough to allow us into the cave. Tomorrow wouldn't be soon enough for me."

14

The following day, the sun shone from a wide blue sky dotted with fleecy white clouds. But the speed at which those clouds moved, and the way the heather bent and the smoke from Willie Meenie's chimney was snatched away was indication enough that the sea was too agitated for cave exploration on Sgarbeg. David watched the signs with a worried frown.

"Will it *ever* be calm enough?" he wondered when he joined Sandy in the kitchen.

"Oh aye," But she didn't sound as hopeful as her words suggested. "The first calm day, we take off, whether we're supposed to be working or not. We'll think of some excuse. Mrs. MacAllister won't mind. Did you see this?"

She handed him a note, written hastily on castle notepaper.

Called away. Will be back for the evening meal. M. Marsh.

"Where did you find this?"

"At the front desk. I don't know when he left. Some time before six this morning."

"Hmm. Maybe to try out the boat he hired."

"If so I hope he's a good sailor. What do you have to do today?"

"Gardening this morning. Then I have to go to town for some supplies for Mrs. MacAllister. Are all the other guests coming down for breakfast?"

"Yes. We have kippers especially for the Wades. Otherwise the usual."

The usual was hot steaming porridge, cold cereal, bacon and eggs and fried potato scones, tea and coffee and lots of toast and jam. Ramshaw guests seldom wanted more for lunch than a little fruit and a cup of tea. The Cadeaus were the exception. This morning they were down first, wide awake and ready to head south to hike in the Harris hills. They ate with healthy and appreciative appetites, then ordered a substantial lunch to be packed and taken with them.

Cliff Turner was right behind them. He headed for the coffee pot as he shrugged into a jacket. He looked around.

"Is Mike Marsh down yet?"

"He's gone, " said Sandy briefly.

"Gone?"

"He left some time before I got up — before six. He won't be back all day."

"Hmm." Cliff looked thoughtful as he poured a cup of coffee. "I'll just have some bacon and eggs, and another coffee to go." He glanced at his watch. "I'll be away all day too. Business in town." He looked at Sandy and David. "How about you two? Are you on duty today?"

"Aye, the usual guided tours. You'll not be wanting your porridge? Och, that's a shame. It'll warm your innards and stick to your ribs. Well, here's your bacon and eggs."

"That will do fine. My "innards" are warm enough, thank you." He ate hurriedly, glancing from time to time at his watch. He was about to leave when the Wades arrived, sniffing the air appreciatively.

"Ah, kippers! That delightful aroma woke us up, didn't it, 'Enery?"

"I'm not surprised." Cliff made a wry face, winked at Sandy, and left.

While the Wades feasted on their fish David joined Sandy in the kitchen.

"Why," he mused, "do you suppose Cliff Turner was interested in what we're doing today?"

Sandy nodded. "I wondered about that too. Davie, do you think we're getting too paranoid? Are we seeing threats where there are none? You know, he may just be innocently interested."

"Yes, I know. That's likely it. All the same I think we'd better keep on being suspicious of everyone. I notice you didn't tell him I would be going into town."

"No, he doesn't have to know everything." She began to fill the sink with hot water. "Don't be too long away, Davie." She hesitated, looking at him, suddenly shy. "I get worried when you're not around — ever since the shooting."

He didn't say anything for a moment. He looked into her eyes and saw a tear there, just for a moment, before she blinked it away. He was suddenly angry — angry at whoever was threatening their lives, threatening *her* life . . .

"I won't be too long, Sandy," he said simply. He picked up a dish towel.

"There's one thing you can do in town." She sank a pile of plates into the sudsy water. "Go to the docks, find Alec, and ask when this wind will blow itself out. He's better than the weather bureau." She glanced out the window. "It's already easing off. We may just make it tomorrow, Davie."

* * *

Lunch was over when David finally went in to Stornoway. He made several purchases for Mrs. MacAllister, then drove to the docks. A quick look along the line of moored boats told him that the *Maisie* was not there. He hailed a man working on the deck of a trawler.

"I'm looking for Alec MacAllister. Have you seen him?"

"Alec? Oh aye." The man straightened and wiped his brow with a paint-stained cloth. "He took a couple of tourists out for a ride. They wanted to see this Death Island they'd heard about." He laughed sardonically. "Alec was quite happy to go as long as they paid well and didn't want to go ashore. That was all right. They just wanted a few pictures to take back home to the States." He squinted skyward to locate the sun. "Should be back soon, I'd say." He pointed to the end of the jetty. "You'll see him coming around the point any time now."

"Okay, thanks."

So Archie's death had revived the legend of Death Island to the point where it was becoming a tourist attraction. I hope, thought David, it doesn't become so popular that we don't have a chance to sneak into the cave without drawing a lot of attention. He walked slowly along the wharf and sat on a bollard to wait.

He didn't have to wait long. A few minutes later he saw a masthead moving beyond the ridge that sheltered the harbour. Then the *Maisie* appeared, swinging into the channel, heading for her berth.

David couldn't have told anyone what made him sense that something was wrong. Perhaps it was the lack of motion on the part of the couple on deck. They were sitting close together on deck chairs, the only amenities aboard the *Maisie*, quite still, holding hands tightly. And as the boat pulled in to the dock he could see that they were white-faced and tense. Perhaps it was the shapeless thing on the deck, covered by a tarpaulin. Or was it the grim look on Alec's face as he expertly nudged his boat alongside the wharf, then stepped out of the wheelhouse and tossed a line to David?

David dropped the eye of the hawser over the bollard, then stepped forward to help the lady onto the wharf. She didn't say anything, moving as if in shock. The man, with a camera slung about his neck, cast one look — of revulsion, it seemed to David — at the thing on the deck, then with one hand on David's shoulder, stepped ashore.

"Death Island," he said grimly, "has claimed another victim."

"What?" David was shocked.

"Another victim." The man jerked his thumb toward the tarpaulin. Then he took the lady's arm, and turned to Alec. "You have our names if we're needed as witnesses. And our hotel."

"Aye. You go along." Alec was seeing to his stern line. He tightened it down then turned to David.

"But who — what — ?" David was bewildered. "What happened?"

"We were sailing down the east coast of Sgarbeg, so they could take a picture of the castle, you see. We saw a boat smashed up on the rocks. It was him." Alec nodded toward the tarpaulin. "Head smashed in — though he wasn't quite dead when we reached him."

"But . . . " David looked out beyond the harbour mouth. There were whitecaps, all right, but the waves didn't seem to be all that big. "Is it that rough out there? Rough enough to toss a boat onto the rocks?"

"Oh, aye — if you're inexperienced, and crippled to boot. Some silly fools have no respect for the sea. They think it's like sailing on a river or a mill pond. . . . "

But David had caught one word, and his heart skipped a beat with sudden foreboding.

"Did you say crippled?"

"Aye, you know him. You'd better take a look."

David hesitated, looking uneasily at the thing on the deck. Then he pulled back one corner of the tarp. That was all he needed. There was no mistaking that face. He covered it up again.

"It's Mike Marsh." David's voice cracked. "A guest at the castle."

"Aye, I recognized him. Saw him when I went to the castle to fetch Martha. Thought he looked familiar then but couldn't place him. Still can't."

"You said he wasn't quite dead when you reached him?"

"That's right, though you couldn't be nearer death's door without going through. He opened his eyes, just a blink, and said 'please' — soft and drawn out like, so it sounded like 'police'. Then he was gone. Which reminds me — accident or no, the police have to be told, and my radio is out. Will you give them a call?"

"Oh sure." David ran along the jetty, his mind in turmoil. Mike Marsh, one of their suspects,

115

was dead. *Was* it an accident? Had the dead man's last word been, in fact, "police?" Had Mike been telling them he had been murdered? Whatever it was, it seemed to David that the elimination of one suspect only confused matters more. . . .

"Hello. Can I speak to Sergeant Hummock?" How would *he* like this development? "Oh. Will you give him a message? This is David McCrimmon from Ramshaw Castle. Tell him one of our guests — Mike Marsh — is dead. An accident, we think . . . thank you."

David hung up the phone and rejoined Alec on the *Maisie*. "Sergeant Hummock wasn't there but I left a message. Maybe they'll send someone else." He shook his head in frustration. "And it may take a while — I just realized I forgot to tell them where we are. They'll go all the way to the castle first."

"No matter." Alec struck a match and puffed his pipe into life. He looked again at the inert shape on the deck. "*He's* not going anywhere." He looked at David, his face serious. "I'm not a great believer of tales of curses and such, lad. I'm not superstitious. But anyone who goes out to Death Island for no reason is asking for trouble."

In other words, thought David, you *are* superstitious. Well, I'm not, and we have good reason for going out there. "What do you think the weather'll be like tomorrow, Alec?"

"Tomorrow?" He looked at the sky and sniffed

the wind. "Yon fool should have waited another day to take his boat out. Tomorrow the Minch will be as calm as it ever will be."

* * *

A few minutes later, as David started his car to return to the castle, Sergeant Hummock's squad car slewed to a stop by the jetty. *He's* no believer of superstitions and curses anyway, thought David. But will he accept "accident" this time?

15

The *White Swan* ploughed into the dead-calm waters of the Minch. A white moustache piled up in front of its blunt bow, then rolled back and spread out in an ever-widening swath, to finally fade and merge with the trackless sea. Bubbles and froth marked the revolutions of the labouring propeller, pushing the old lugger away from the shores of Lewis.

Sandy was at the wheel, whistling cheerily. The bow was pointed towards the distant, whale-like island. An occasional adjustment of the wheel countered the northward push of the unseen fingers of the Gulf Stream. It was *too* calm — Sandy would have preferred some motion, some struggle, some more life to the slumbering sea. But this was what they had been waiting for.

David roamed the deck. He dodged the opening in the middle of the deck, checked the slanting mast to see if it was as unstable as it looked.

He watched the lazily breaking furrows, the writhing wake, the far-flung islands scattered across the sea. He watched two workmanlike fishing boats away to the north. He studied with envy the graceful white *Kittiwake*, sails down, moving under power on an oblique path that would eventually carry her across their bows. He moved to the apex of the bow to watch the gradually approaching Sgarbeg.

And it vanished before his startled eyes.

For a moment he gaped in astonishment. Then he watched in nervous fascination as a white cloud swept in towards them, swallowing the fishing boats, the *Kittiwake*, closing in to wrap a moist, impenetrable shroud around the *White Swan*.

He turned. Wisps of vapour curled around the mast, and the wheelhouse was an illusory shadow in the swirling haze.

He stumbled back, avoiding the black hole in the deck, to the door of the wheelhouse.

"Sandy! Look at that fog! What do we do now?"

"We keep going," said Sandy calmly. "A little slower, maybe, though we haven't been breaking any speed limits." She cut back on the throttle and the noise of the engine subsided to about half its former clatter. "We have a use for Noah's compass after all. And the foghorn."

"Foghorn! Oh no, not that," pleaded David in mock horror. "Be sure to warn me before you blast away on it."

"Aye, I'll give you lots of warning. We won't have to use it for a while. There's no traffic nearby. The *Kittiwake* is the closest, and on her present course it will be half an hour before we get near her." She glanced at her watch. "Fifteen minutes to be safe, then we'll sound the horn at regular intervals. Keep watch, Davie. The fog will probably lighten now and then, and you'll be able to see a bit before it closes in again. But your ears will be more important than your eyes."

"Aye aye, sir. What about radar? Most ships have it now, don't they?"

"I'm sure the *Kittiwake* has, so we won't have to worry about her anyway. It'll be at least an hour before we get close to Sgarbeg. The fog will likely have lifted by then."

Likely, but not certainly. David thought of those cruel cliffs, of the rock teeth thrusting up through the surface just off the coast. He thought of Death Island suddenly looming up out of the fog, too late for the old engine to pull them back. At least, he told himself, the sea was calm. It wouldn't smash them to pieces as it had done to Archie and his boat.

All the same it was unnerving. It was like being blind, groping ahead into that opaque vapour. All sense of direction was gone. They could have been heading back to Lewis for all they could tell.

He squeezed into the wheelhouse and looked over Sandy's shoulder. "It's a good thing we have that compass, even if it is an antique."

"Aye. Would you like to steer for a while? It's not like the gyro compass on the *Bochan*. There are no degrees marked on it. Just keep the lubber's line on east by north and we'll be all right."

She moved aside to let him take her place. "Keep an eye on your watch. In ten minutes we'll have a go on the foghorn — listen."

A sound came through the white blanket: a long, mournful groan. It was answered almost at once by another, higher-pitched.

"Now that," said David, "is more my idea of what a foghorn should sound like. That'll be the fishing boats, right?"

"Aye. They'll be anxious. They weren't far apart."

"If I hadn't known they were away off to the north I couldn't have told you which direction the sound came from."

"No. Fog distorts sound sometimes. But we'll know if one comes close. I'm away for a walk around the deck."

He watched her as she approached the bow. By the time she reached the mast she was already indistinct, like a wraith walking in a cloud, while the fishing boats kept tabs on each other with their cautionary soundings. She came back to the wheelhouse.

"All right," she said. "Hang on to your hat. I'm going to sound the horn."

Siren would have been a more appropriate term than horn. But this time David was ready for it, and perhaps the fog deadened it. At any rate the short, sharp, "whoop" had lost its bite. David was about to comment on it when he realized that Sandy was listening, tense.

After a long moment she shook her head. "I thought the *Kittiwake* would answer."

"Maybe because he has us on radar he doesn't think it necessary."

"He should answer anyway. He must know *we* don't have it and will want to know where he is. That's common courtesy." She reached up and turned the handle again, and kept turning it to produce a long wail that rose and fell.

Again there was no answer.

Sandy frowned. "He should know how to behave in a fog. He's been around here long enough."

"I thought you sailors always referred to boats and ships as 'she'. How come you're calling the *Kittiwake* 'he'?"

"I wasn't thinking of the yacht. I was thinking of the owner. Or his captain. He has a crew to run her for him."

She left him again and took another turn around the deck. When she returned she tried the horn once more.

There was still no answer.

"Maybe they've gone the other way," suggested David.

Her only answer was a frown and a shake of her head. She drifted to the bow again, and he could tell that she was listening intently.

When she came back she reached into the corner of the wheelhouse and handed him a life jacket. She smiled in answer to his raised eyebrows. "Just a precaution," she said lightly, donning her own. "You never know, in a fog . . . "

David felt a finger of alarm crawl up the back of his neck. "Think we should stop and wait for it to lift?"

"Aye — well, almost." She adjusted the throttle to a low murmur. "We'll just keep enough way on so we don't drift."

The engine noise was only an undertone now, the wake barely perceptible. Only the eerie dirge of the distant foghorns broke the silence. The fog hung oppressively over them, opaque, intimidating.

Now and then Sandy sounded their own horn. There was no reply. The *Kittiwake* was out there, somewhere. But where? Why didn't she answer?

Sandy paced the deck nervously, stopping to listen, going to the bow to peer helplessly ahead. David stayed at the wheel. It was only a matter of holding it steady now, but he couldn't leave it. He too stared, and listened. There shouldn't be anything to worry about. The *Kittiwake* was far enough away. And she had radar. Nevertheless he *was* worried. Largely because he sensed that Sandy was worried too.

The *Kittiwake*. He remembered her, offshore, while he and Sandy ran Alec MacAllister's dinghy up the length of Sgarbeg. He remembered the man on the deck watching through binoculars. She was there too, when they emerged from the cave. . . .

She was there! How much had the man with the glasses seen? Would that explain . . . ?

He got no further. His thoughts were shattered by a scream.

Sandy was at the mast, yelling at him, pointing helplessly into the fog.

For a moment he could see nothing. Then suddenly there was a shadow, looming out of the fog. A shadow that became the prow of a ship, towering over them.

A moment of frozen horror. Then he swung the wheel, desperately. But he could feel something giving way. The helm didn't answer.

He watched, rivetted in shock, and saw it happen as if in slow motion: the bow striking the lugger, catapulting Sandy over the side; the *White Swan* disintegrating, timbers shattering, deck tilting and rending, mast collapsing into the water. Then he was hurled from the wheelhouse. It hung over him as the doomed lugger heaved up, sending him sprawling, grasping at something — anything — solid.

He saw the phantom ship slice through the wreckage, silent, remorseless. There was a man looking down at him from her deck, watching the carnage, uncaring. Then it was gone, as suddenly and silently as it had come. And David was sliding helplessly into the sea.

16

David was alone in a close, silent world; alone except for scattered wreckage, all that remained of the *White Swan*.

He was aware only of the cold water, the buoyancy of his life jacket, and the oppressive fog. Visibility extended only a few metres in all directions with no discernible horizon, for the sea and fog merged to become one. And the only sound was the faraway lament of the foghorns.

And he was thinking only of one thing: that moment when the ghost ship swept out of the fog and struck the lugger. He had had a brief glimpse of Sandy being hurled over the side, and then she was gone, lost behind the relentless vessel. She had been wearing a life jacket — she must be all right. She *had* to be all right.

"Sandy!" he shouted. "Sandy!"

A moment of silence, an interminable moment, then a voice came thinly through the fog.

"Davie! I'm here. Are you all right?"

Thank God! "Yes, I'm fine." He stared hopefully into the surrounding pall. From which direction had the voice come? It was impossible to tell.

"I can't see you," he shouted. "Keep yelling, Sandy. I can't tell where you are."

"You shout too," she called back. There, was that her head, buoyed up by her jacket? No, just another piece of wreckage from the lugger. "Sandy, *m'eudail*, where are you?"

There was another moment of silence, then her voice came again. She was singing. The lugger was gone, the fog hung thick all around and they were an unknown number of miles from land, but she was singing. Then she stopped.

"Am I any closer?"

"Yes. I know where you are now. I'm coming!"

She resumed her song. "The Lord's my shepherd, I'll not want . . . " Suddenly her voice was very close. And there she was, emerging out of the vapour.

They saw each other at the same time and reached out into a close embrace — as close as their bulky life jackets permitted.

"Sandy!" he breathed in relief.

She pushed back and looked into his face. "What do we do now, Sandy?" he said. "Will they be looking for us? That ship — they *know* they ran us down. There was a man on the deck and he saw it all. But he didn't *do* anything."

"Perhaps he didn't have time. It was so sudden." But her voice lacked conviction. "Did you recognize her, Davie? That was the *Kittiwake*, you know."

"The *Kittiwake*?" It had seemed like a monster, much larger than the white yacht. But of course he had never been *that* close to her before. "Why didn't they answer our foghorn? Why didn't they have us on radar? You'd almost think . . . " His voice trailed off. She finished for him.

" . . . that she ran us down on purpose. Yes, that's exactly what I thought. But that's impossible."

"It's crazy," agreed David. "It must be that it happened so fast there was nothing they could do about it, like you said."

"But then, why haven't they come back to rescue us?"

"Maybe they're still coming. They'd have to stop and swing around and we'll be hard to find in this fog. They'll be afraid of running us down again."

"So they would make a noise, wouldn't they? If their foghorn isn't working they'd calling out to us. That's what anyone else would do. I don't think they're coming, Davie."

"Wait a minute. There! Isn't that a boat?"

Something was materializing out of the mist, something floating on the surface and bigger than any remnant of the *White Swan*. Something pointed, like the bow of a boat.

"But there's no one in it." said David, wonderingly.

"Of course not," said Sandy in excitement. "It's our raft. It must have inflated automatically, as it's supposed to do when it hit the water. I forgot all about it. Come on."

They reached for it. Sandy caught the rope around the gunwale. "Give me a boost, Davie."

"Okay. Bend your knees." He reached into the water for her feet. "Right. When I say Go. Ready? Go!" He lifted with an effort that forced him under the surface. When he came up she was half on board, squirming to pull her legs over the side.

"Now it's your turn." She reached for him. With her help he was able to hook one leg over the gunwale but this threatened to upset the raft. She had to sit back quickly to right it. But he was able to grasp the rope and in another moment he rolled onto the bottom of the boat.

It wasn't very big, but it was made of heavy, coated rubber and there were paddles with wooden handles and plastic blades.

"It's not the *Kittiwake*," he said, sitting up. "But it's dry, and we can get moving."

"Yes we can," acknowledged Sandy. "But we won't. Not yet. We're not far from Sgarbeg but I have no idea which direction to go."

"No, I suppose not." He looked helplessly into the heavy curtain that still hung all around. "Oh, for a compass. Even Noah's reject. And I wouldn't mind having a foghorn either. I wonder where the *Kittiwake* is now. Sandy," he said, frowning, "remember when we went into the cave?"

"Yes?"

"Remember where the *Kittiwake* was? She was right there. Well, not *right* there, but she wasn't far away, and there was a man on her deck watching us through binoculars. Suppose that man was Cliff Turner?"

She sat very still, comprehension dawning in her eyes.

"Yes! That would explain — that would explain a lot. He saw us coming out of the cave. He thought we might have taken pictures — he might even have seen the flash. There was something in there he didn't want us to see, so he followed us to find out if we had actually seen it. He saw you with the pictures, and when you left them in the car he took the one — and the negative — that might give him away. Then he took a room at the castle to keep an eye on us. Perhaps he was looking for a chance to — to rig an accident."

"And he followed us to Callanish," continued David. "He took a shot at us. If he killed us it would look like a "random thing," as he called it. There would be no reason to connect him with it. But the police car came along and scared him off. We were lucky. He said that himself, remember? And today he saw another opportunity, and took it: the *Kittiwake* came along and ran us down in the fog."

"But when did he board her? He spent the night at the castle. He would have had to have left before we did this morning — and then how would he know we would be out here? How did he know about the lugger? It isn't as if we set out from Stornoway, where everyone would see us."

"I don't know. . . . " David frowned. "Remember that man who watched us when we were looking the *White Swan* over? Could that have been Cliff Turner? Remember, you said he looked familiar."

She paused, thinking back. "I suppose . . . I think he was shorter than Cliff, but at that distance I could be wrong. Look, however it came about, if they did run us down deliberately, what will they do next?"

David looked around uneasily. There could be anything out there, waiting for the fog to clear. "They know they hit us, but they couldn't be sure if we went down with the ship or not. I saw a man on the deck — if he saw me he probably saw that I was wearing a life jacket. So they might be back to make sure of us. Could they find their way back to this spot?"

"I don't know. I don't think they would pick us up on radar." She began to unship the paddles. "All the same I think we should get away from here. If they do come back and find the wreckage but no sign of us they might think we've drowned and give up. They can't know about the raft."

"Right." David grabbed one of the paddles.

"Which way?"

"It doesn't matter as long as we leave the remains of the *White Swan* behind."

They began to paddle. The raft was light and moved easily, and in no time the last vestige of lugger had vanished into the fog.

"We might as well keep going," said David. "The exercise feels good. That water was cold. And the farther we get from the wreckage the better." He looked back at their wake. "We aren't going in circles, are we?"

"I don't think so. We're matching stroke for stroke so we should be keeping a pretty straight course. Of course we might end up in Ireland."

"Good," said David lightly. "I've never been to Ireland. Just so we don't bump into the *Kittiwake*."

It was some time later, there was no telling how long, when Sandy suddenly whispered, "Look, Davie. Look ahead, at the water. Do you see what I see?"

He looked, and shook his head. "I don't know what you see. All I see is the sea."

"But don't you see more of it than a little while ago? Look. The fog is lifting!"

"Oh! I think you're right! It is!" He pulled his paddle in. "This is going to be interesting. We'll soon know where we are. Will we see Ireland, Lewis or just an endless expanse of ocean?"

She laughed, a little uneasily. "We haven't gone *that* far. The only thing that concerns me is, will we see the *Kittiwake*? And will she see us? And if so what will she do about it?"

They waited tensely, but not for long. Once it started the fog dissipated rapidly. Suddenly there was a dark shadow materializing out of the vapours; a dark shadow that expanded and spread out before them and towered above them, only metres away. In another few minutes they would have run right into it.

"It's Sgarbeg!" cried Sandy, unbelieving. "Davie, it's Sgarbeg!"

Sgarbeg. Death Island . . .

17

David looked up at the emerging hills, then around at the ever-widening circle of water. He grabbed his paddle.

"What do you think, Sandy?"

"I think we'd better go ashore before the *Kittiwake* shows up."

"Right, I think so too. We've got to find a place to land. Do you know this side of the island?"

"Aye. There's an inlet along here somewhere." They paddled furiously, while every detail of the land grew more distinct with the evaporation of the mists. The heights above rose, then fell, then rose again, and suddenly plunged to the water's edge in a dark, narrow defile.

"This is it." They swung the raft in through the opening, into a pool that moved in a slow circle at the foot of a tall white waterfall. The hills rose precipitously on all sides except for one spot where a short stretch of sand lay at the foot of a steep slope.

"We'll beach there," decided David. He looked back over his shoulder. "It looks as if the raft will be hidden from seaward by the curve of the land if we leave it there."

"Good. We'll be safe here. We can't do anything till the fog lifts. And I guess what we do then depends on the *Kittiwake*."

"Right." They paddled over to the sand, stepped out and pulled the raft above the high-water mark.

"Now." David looked up to the cliff top high above, then to Sandy. "We have to get up there so we can see what's going on. How are you at climbing?"

"I'm no expert, but I think I can manage this slope all right. I'll go first so you can catch me if I slip."

"Okay. But I strongly recommend you slip as little as possible. We both might end up back down here."

"What we need," said Sandy, "is a positive attitude. We *will* climb to the top. All the same, I'll go first."

David grinned. "And I *will* catch you if you slip. And we *won't* end up back down here. We'll make it to the top, without a doubt, and all our problems will be solved — sooner or later."

"That's the spirit! Let's go."

The first part was easy enough, but then the gradient steepened. Stones loosened under their feet and tumbled down beneath them. Vegetation came free in their hands from tenuous holds in rock crevices. Sneaker toes sought for niches and slipped on smooth rock faces. At one point Sandy failed to find a hold on a steep incline, and began to slide helplessly backward. David caught her, scrabbling desperately for a foothold, knees scraping over jagged stones, fingers clutching at anything that would hold. They stopped, flat against the ground.

"There!" said David, breathlessly, "I told you we wouldn't end up at the bottom. We didn't lose more than a metre."

"Right! A positive attitude will do it every time." She looked at her hands ruefully, then at her torn jeans. "What are a few cuts and bruises in the whole scheme of life? Let's go. Onward and upward."

"I think," suggested David, "that a diagonal approach might be the best for the next few yards. There's a particularly ugly stretch up ahead that we're definitely not shod to cope with."

"I know. I've got my eye on it. Don't worry, I've got our path picked out. Just follow me and I won't lead you astray. Close your eyes if you like and hang on to my heel."

"Right. I'll do that. Lead on, Macduff."

He didn't close his eyes, but he let her choose the way, and his trust was justified. They reached the top at last, rolled over the crest, and lay for a moment to catch their breath.

They sat up again almost at once. David inspected the tear in the left knee of his jeans, and brushed dirt out of the ugly scrape beneath. Then he turned to Sandy. "Are you okay? No serious loss of blood?"

"Nothing that an immediate transfusion wouldn't cure." Her hands were the worst, both abraded. "If my mother were here she could kiss them better."

"Well, in the absence of your mother, I could have a go at it." He caught her hands and brushed them gently with his lips, then looked up into her face. "Have I a mother's touch?"

She laughed. "No, definitely not. But it was nice of you to try." She got to her feet and pulled him up beside her and they looked around.

Visibility was widening perceptibly. The whole island was revealed, with the exception of the cliff tops at the northern end where tendrils of mist still lingered. The seascape too was broadening on all sides, but as yet there was nothing out there but water.

"It'll soon be gone," she said. "Then we'll be able to see what the *Kittiwake* is up to. Let's go to the castle. It's on the highest point of land. We'll have the best view from there."

"Good idea."

Not much was left of the ancient curtain wall that had once enclosed the castle grounds. Here and there a wall stood to shoulder height, the last vestige, perhaps, of the chapel, the kitchen or the brewhouse. But the keep itself still stood, square and solid, its outer wall merging with the cliff and sweeping in an unbroken plane to the sea far below. David looked up to the top of the tower, where corbelled turrets graced each corner.

"Can we go up there?" he asked. "That would be the perfect lookout place if the stairs are still intact."

"Oh aye, stone staircases don't decay. Let's go."

Steps, worn in the middle by countless feet over hundreds of years, led upwards through the middle of the incredibly thick walls. There were also steps leading down, into darkness, into the very bowels of the cliff itself.

"What's down there?" wondered David. "Dungeons?"

"Dungeons," confirmed Sandy, "and storerooms. The lairds used to be paid in kind rather than cash. Cattle or crops or whatever the people had to pay their rents with. So the laird needed lots of storage space."

"Someday," said David, "we'll come back and explore down there. Right now I guess we'd better go up."

There was a landing at each storey, marked by arrow slits and gun loops on the outer walls, and by a doorway on the inner side opening onto space where there were once wooden floors, long since crumbled into dust. They climbed to the top, into the open, where a walkway led all around the four sides of the keep. From one of the corner turrets they had an uninterrupted view in all directions. In the short time it had taken them to climb to the top the fog had dissipated entirely.

"There she is." Sandy pointed, excitedly. The unmistakable white yacht rode like a graceful swan on the cobalt sea, several miles away. She was unmoving, apparently hove-to.

"Isn't that just about where she hit us?" wondered David.

"I would think so," nodded Sandy. "I wish we had some binoculars. Look, there's another boat with her. A small one. A motor launch. I wonder what's going on."

"Perhaps they reported the collision. They would have to, wouldn't they? There must have been some damage to their bow when they hit us. Someone would ask questions about that sooner or later."

"Oh aye, they'll report it. An accident in the fog. Faulty radar. Terribly remorseful. Don't know what they hit. Searching for survivors, if any. They'll report it all right. In fact I expect that's the police launch there with them now."

"And all they'll find is wreckage. Maybe enough to identify the lugger, maybe not. And nobody knows we were using it."

"*Somebody* knows," corrected Sandy. "If we were run down on purpose someone *must* have known."

"Our friend Mr. Turner." David nodded. "You

know, he needn't have been aboard at all. He could have followed us this morning, then notified the *Kittiwake* by radio that we were heading out."

"Aye, and we can be sure *he* won't tell anyone we were the ones who were shipwrecked. They'll find out eventually, of course, through Jemmie Macdonald, but that will take time. We might be here for quite a while, Davie."

"We'll see what happens when the *Kittiwake* leaves. I don't feel like paddling our raft all the way back home, but there'll be lots of ships in sight before long. We should be able to signal or paddle out to meet one. Preferably that police launch, if that's what it is."

There *was* more and more traffic in sight. The two fishing boats that had communicated with each other by foghorn were still there, away to the north, and another one could be seen beating its way seaward from the mainland. It seemed to David that there was some activity in the direction of Stornoway, but that was too far away to tell for sure. Nothing was approaching Sgarbeg. Not that it mattered. They daren't show themselves as long as the *Kittiwake* was in sight.

Several minutes passed before it became evident that the yacht was underway. She moved in a wide circle, then pulled away, leaving the smaller craft behind. David watched it for a moment, then turned to Sandy in alarm. "She's coming *this* way. You don't suppose they're coming to Sgarbeg, do you?"

"Not likely. I expect she's just making for home." She turned to look back to where the mainland was low on the horizon, below cloud-topped hills. "She may be heading for Ullapool. Once she's past us and the island is between her and the police we'll try to attract attention."

The *Kittiwake* came on, bows on to the island. Then she swung a point or two to the north, on a course that would take her past the northern cliffs.

"She's going to be close," warned Sandy. "Probably on purpose. They can't be certain that we didn't make it here, so they'll be on the lookout. We'd better keep down."

The castle parapets were made for lookouts. They watched the approaching ship through the embrasures.

"Look at that," whispered Sandy. "she's been damaged all right. If the sea weren't so calm she'd have to go astern." As it was the crushed bow was safely clear of the water that curled back before her steady advance. As she drew closer they could see a man on her foredeck, scanning the heights through binoculars. They crouched low behind the merlons. Then Sandy risked a quick look.

The *Kittiwake* had passed so close to the island that now she was hidden below the cliffs. Her approach had startled hundreds of birds who exploded from their nests and hung in a scream-

141

ing cloud around the cliff tops.

"She's out of sight," said Sandy, "but be careful. She'll be out the other side in a minute."

But she wasn't. One minute passed. Two, then three. They exchanged puzzled glances. "What happened? Where'd she go?"

"Wait! There she is now!"

The yacht reappeared. She had slowed to a crawl, and had changed direction, so that she was moving down the east coast of the island, close inshore. David frowned.

"I don't like this," he muttered. "D'you suppose they're heading for the landing place? D'you think they're going to come ashore?"

"Maybe." Sandy watched the yacht nervously. "They're out of sight of the police now, so maybe they're going to make a quick search of the island just in case we made it this far. And if they do, and look down into the inlet where we landed, they'll see our raft and they'll *know* we're here somewhere. And they'll find us."

"The police! We've got to try to attract the police. I *hope* that's a police launch out there."

"It's a long way off," said Sandy doubtfully. "But we'd better try. The *Kittiwake* people won't dare harm us if they see the police launch approaching. Come on. We'd better go to the cliff top and wave something. Your shirt. My sweater. Anything."

"Look!" David pointed. "I think the launch is coming this way. They may see us yet. Let's go."

They ran down the four flights of stairs, across the ancient courtyard, over the spine of the island to the cliff top. David tore off his shirt as they ran. Yes, the police boat was definitely headed towards the island, but slowly. Much too slowly. They stopped at the cliff top and David began to wave his shirt frantically.

Sandy pulled her sweater over her head. "I hope Sergeant Hummock's awake," she said "He's still quite a long way off."

David hesitated. "Sergeant Hummock. D'you think that's him out there?"

"Oh aye, it's him all right. He's always the one on the launch. Come on, Davie, keep waving." She began to swing her sweater from side to side. "Davie?"

David was suddenly still. Sergeant Hummock? He remembered the policeman, coming to their rescue at Callanish, and again that evening when he had come in to the castle when the guests had gathered for evening tea. He had said something then that had bothered David, that had nagged at him, that somehow hadn't been *right*. What was it?

"Davie, what is it? Don't quit now. I *think* they've spotted us but we can't be sure."

Then he remembered. "No. Wait! Sandy! I don't think we want Sergeant Hummock at all."

"Don't want him! What are you talking about! We *need* him, Davie. Those *Kittiwake* people will be here in a few minutes."

"That can't be helped," said David, suddenly grim. "We don't want Sergeant Hummock because *he's one of them*. He's the one who tried to kill us at Callanish!"

18

She stared at him, open-mouthed.

"Davie! What are you talking about? That's crazy! He *rescued* us!"

"Think! That night when he came into the castle where we were all having tea. Do you remember what he said? I said I had seen the man who shot at us — "

"And that was Sergeant Hummock? Then why — ?"

"No, no, I only saw a shadow — I couldn't tell who it was. But listen — Sergeant Hummock said, 'Was that before or after you two separated?' Sandy, how did he know we separated? We never told him — we only showed him where we had been standing when the shot was fired. The only person who could have known what happened after is the person who was shooting at us!"

"But how — you can't be sure — I can't believe

that! He might have assumed . . . There must be some other explanation. Or why would he rescue us? It doesn't make sense."

"Yes it does. Someone saw him there. Someone saw the police car, anyway. So he had to start acting like a policeman, to divert suspicion."

"But that someone was Cliff Turner, and *he's* got to be one of them too."

"I know. I don't understand everything, but I'm certain that Hummock is on their side. That's not the only mistake he made. The morning Mike Marsh was brought in, I left a message for Sergeant Hummock but forgot to say where I was. Yet Sergeant Hummock was at the docks in a few minutes. Why did he go right there and not to the castle? Sandy, I don't want him to see us. Maybe we can hide from the *Kittiwake*. They don't know for sure we're here."

"Unless they see our raft," she reminded him. "And we're too late anyway." She pointed out over the water. The launch was aproaching fast, spreading a seething wake far astern. "He'll be here soon. And so will the *Kittiwake*. It's too late — wait a minute!" She was pointing again, to the northwest. There was a lobster boat out there, heading directly for Sgarbeg. "That's the *Maisie*," she said, excited. "Alec MacAllister's boat. I know it by the wheelhouse."

It was still a long way off, and it wasn't built for speed. The police launch, on the other hand . . .

"D'you think Alec's coming here?" wondered David, hardly daring to hope. "Why would he be coming to Sgarbeg?"

"Someone might have hired him. He's certainly headed this way. If we can hide out till he gets here no one's going to harm us in front of him and his passengers. They'll want it to appear accidental. Won't they?"

"I hope so," said David grimly. "He's our only hope anyway. Let's go. I think the dungeons are our best bet."

They hesitated at the top of the steps. The dozen they could see led down into nothing but darkness. They looked at each other mutely, and joined hands. Without a word they descended into a black void. They stopped again, when there were no more steps, and waited for their eyes to adjust. It made little difference. There was no telling what lay ahead of them.

"You were here once before?" asked David. He was whispering. It seemed the natural thing to do. "What's down here?"

"Nothing much, as far as I remember. There's a hallway with rooms off to each side. The first two are dungeons. There used to be yetts — iron barricades — but they're gone. There are two more rooms beyond the dungeons. Storerooms. Empty, except for a stone slab in one of them that was used as a table. There's nowhere to hide, if they've got lights. And there's no other way out."

She shivered. It was cold and dank. "We'll be trapped, Davie."

Trapped! David was suddenly sweating in spite of the cold. His mind raced over the other possibilities. There were none; none that he knew of.

"Have we any choice?" he asked. "There's the house. They'll be sure to search that first. There's nowhere else, is there?"

She shook her head reluctantly. "No. Everything else is wide open. We can't climb down to the caves, and there's nowhere to hide in the tower. They'll leave the dungeons till last. If they don't have lights with them, maybe they'll have to go back for them. That will give us a little more time." She shivered again. "You're right. This is our only hope. This and Alec MacAllister. We'll have to ask God to give the *Maisie* a mighty big shove."

David grinned for a moment. "I can just see him, hanging on to the wheel while the *Maisie* takes off like a greyhound." He tried to speak lightly, without much success. "One of us better keep watch so we know what's going on."

"No, we'll *both* keep watch." David didn't argue. They went back up, hand in hand, into the glaring sunlight, and looked out from the castle doorway. From here they could see the *Maisie*, still coming, but still a long way off. The island itself was deserted. There was no sign of life.

"I wish I knew what was going on," muttered David, uneasily. "The *Kittiwake* must have docked by now."

"Maybe they're waiting for the launch to arrive," suggested Sandy. "Whether Sergeant Hummock is with them or not he will have radioed that he saw us."

The launch was no longer in sight. It would be below the cliffs by now. It would have to go around the south of Sgarbeg and back up to the wharf. Meanwhile the *Maisie* was drawing closer. Gradually.

"We could keep watch from the top of the tower," suggested David. "When someone comes ashore we'll have lots of time to get back down to the dungeons."

"Aye. Let's do that."

They climbed back up to the ramparts high atop the old keep. From the battlements they looked straight down hundreds of feet to the sea, lapping somnolently against the foot of the cliffs; down where, centuries before, a maiden and her lover had been dashed to pieces, clasped in each other's arms.

And looking southward they saw the *Kittiwake*. She had tied up to the jetty. There appeared to be some movement on her deck but as yet no one had come ashore.

"I expect you're right," said David. "They'll be waiting for the police to arrive."

"You could be wrong about Sergeant Hummock you know, Davie. Maybe they told him they would have a look around here in case we had made it this far. Then when he saw us waving he radioed the *Kittiwake* to let them know we're alive. And since he knows, they can't do anything to us. Don't you think?"

David shook his head stubbornly. "I wish you were right. But I don't think so. Anyway we'll assume he's one of them until we find out differently. That's the only way to be sure." He looked back hopefully towards the distant Outer Isles and the slowly approaching *Maisie*. Alec MacAllister was coming closer. When *he* reached Sgarbeg they wouldn't dare harm Sandy and David. Would they? Or was Alec sailing to his own doom? No, surely not. Not if he had several passengers on board. They couldn't . . . dispose of everyone. They'd want to make it look accidental. Wouldn't they?

Meantime all they could do was wait.

The police launch appeared. It swept in and pulled up beside the *Kittiwake* with a great surge of boiling water at its stern. Sergeant Hummock stepped aboard the yacht. They could see him conferring with two or three men on the foredeck. Still no one came ashore.

"They're waiting for us to go to them," said Sandy. "We would do that if you weren't suspicious of the sergeant."

He looked at her. "I *could* be wrong. Do you want to do that?"

She hesitated. Then she shook her head. "No. I think you're right."

And when they didn't appear? What would they do then? Sooner or later they would come searching. And sooner or later they would be successful. . . . David hugged Sandy's arm closer to him. "I just hope they wait long enough for the *Maisie* to get here. I don't think they have any idea she's coming."

The lobster boat was closer, a small bow wave visible now, as she changed course slightly to go around the northern cliffs. David looked to the *Kittiwake* again. He could see a man in white pants, a blue jacket and a yachting cap standing on her deck, conferring with the sergeant. David turned back to the *Maisie*, only to find she was out of view below the cliffs, where the agitated birds still hung in a swirling cloud. Then she reappeared. She was sailing close inshore, heading for the already crowded wharf. She must have been spotted.

David heaved a sigh of relief. "Good. Now we can walk down there in the open. With Alec and his passengers looking on there won't be anything the others can do about it."

"No! No, we can't." Sandy had caught his arm in dismay. She was pointing downward. "*Look!*" The *Maisie* was directly below them. Alec MacAllister was out of sight in the wheelhouse, and there was only one man on her deck. David and Sandy stared at each other in alarm. "Cliff Turner!" muttered David, white-faced. "I can't believe it! There goes our last hope."

19

Still they waited. What else could they do? Mr. MacAllister was still on the *Maisie*, doubtless with no idea what was going on. Was there any hope there?

"If we could get to the *Maisie* unseen," said David, "we might get away yet."

"How are we going to do that? She'll tie up beside the police launch. That means we'd have to cross two other ships to get to her. Maybe we could swim out to her. But we can't get down to the water without being seen. There's no cover . . ."

Sandy was right. The *Maisie* pulled up beside the launch. Cliff Turner threw a heaving line across to the *Kittiwake* and the lobster boat was secured fore and aft. Alec appeared out of the wheelhouse. He spoke briefly to his passenger, then opened the hatch and disappeared into his tiny cabin.

"He'll be having a nap while Mr. Turner explores the castle," guessed Sandy in a small voice. "He has no idea . . . "

Then, at last, they came ashore: Cliff Turner, Sergeant Hummock and the third man, now carrying a rifle under his arm. Mutely, hands fiercely clasped, David and Sandy watched as the three advanced remorselessly towards the castle. A search of the old cottage took only a few moments. Then the policeman, coming along the far cliff top, spotted the raft below. The others joined him there for a moment, then they came on, spread out. The island lay before them, bare of any possible cover. Except for Sgarbeg Castle.

"Come on, Sandy. The dungeons. It's our only hope now."

Some hope! It was only delaying inevitable capture. And then what? There was no way of knowing, no use speculating. But David's mind raced anyway. They would be made to disappear, so that it would be assumed they had drowned. And the secret of Sgarbeg Island — of Death Island — would never be revealed. Not that that mattered now. In the face of death it no longer mattered . . . .

It was unbelievably dark, and damp, and cold in the tunnel. They felt their way, hands groping the rough, wet walls. A few metres in, and the walls were suddenly no longer there.

"That's the dungeons," said Sandy, shakily, "There's nothing there. Let's keep going."

They edged forward, stumbling over the broken rock floor, hands out to the walls again. Then a few more tentative steps, and once again the walls fell away.

"The store rooms," whispered Sandy. "That one's empty. This one has the stone slab. It's the height of a table. It'll be something to hide behind. It's our only chance."

They turned into the room. It was even darker in here. They wouldn't have believed that possible. They hesitated, stock still. Suddenly there were sounds. Small sounds. Whispers of sounds. The drip of water. The rustle of tiny feet.

"Ooh!" Sandy caught David's arm convulsively. Something ran across their toes.

"Rats," said David weakly. "We'll have to ignore them."

"I *can't*!" Sandy shivered violently. But she crept gingerly forward with him. David had his hands out in front of him. "Here it is. It's a good height. We'll go around it."

They felt their way along it and around to the other side. The doorway into the storage room was outlined faintly by daylight reaching in vainly from the far entrance. They waited, hands clasped desperately, hearts thumping, listening to the scurry of rats and the inevitable approach of their opponents. . . .

It came, at last, after an interminable wait. There was the light first, a wavering light that outlined the doorway, moved across the wall of the alleyway, then dimmed. And voices. Low, unintelligible at first. Then one voice, loud and clear.

"Sandy and David. We know you're in here. Come on out. We're not going to harm you. We're here to take you home."

It was Sergeant Hummock. David squeezed Sandy's hand. "He wouldn't talk that way if he was really here to rescue us. Be ready to duck down."

The light brightened. They heard footsteps. Then the challenge again.

"Come on out. You can't get away. I *told* you to stay away from Sgarbeg. You ought to listen."

Then the light was right there. It swung around and pierced the gloom of the storeroom opposite. Three men stood there, big black shadows obscuring it. David and Sandy crouched down, hard against the stone slab, breath suspended.

Now the light was turned their way. They were aware of it sweeping around the room. It passed over them, came back, lingered above their heads, then moved on, all around the room, like some live thing with an identity of its own. They crouched there in the deep shadow behind the stone table, sweating in fear, waiting; waiting in despair for the light to find them, as surely it must. . . .

The light dimmed. It had been turned away! A man spoke, a voice they didn't recognize.

"They're not here! We missed them somehow. Where else could they be?"

"I don't know." Sergeant Hummock sounded bewildered. "They're here somewhere. I saw them signalling from the cliffs."

"You're absolutely sure you saw them, are you, Sergeant?"

That was Cliff Turner.

"Of course I am! I was sure they would be at the jetty to greet me. They must have become suspicious for some reason. I can't think why."

The three men had turned away. Sandy and David hadn't been seen! Their thumping hearts hadn't been heard! In new-found hope David moved a cramped limb gingerly . . . and froze.

"Just a minute!" Cliff Turner was speaking. "If you're sure they're here someplace, there's one place we haven't looked. Give me the light."

They were coming back! "Stay down!" They had almost won! David wanted to scream in frustration. He bit his lip, hard. There was the light again. Once more it passed over their heads. Footsteps came close, came around the end of the table.

Then abruptly Sandy and David were blinded by the light glaring in their faces. It glinted on the barrel of a gun, pointed at them.

"Well well, what have we here!" said Cliff Turner grimly. "Come on out, you two. Let's go."

* * *

They stumbled up the steps and the glorious Hebridean vista opened up around them. Never had the sea been so alluring, the call of the distant hills so urgent. Never had the heather at their feet been so splendid, or the milling birds so beautiful, the sky so intensely blue.

David felt a lump in his throat. Never had Sandy — with her smudged face and her blue eyes, frightened as his own must be — never had Sandy been so beautiful. Sandy *m'eudail* . . .

He hesitated, his hand clutching hers in desperation. The revolver prodded against his spine. "Keep moving."

"Wait a minute!" The man in the yachting clothes held up his hand. "We have to decide what we're going to do. We reported that we ran down a lugger in the fog. It was an accident. There'll be a lot of questions but no one will be able to prove otherwise. We'll get away with it all right. Sooner or later, Sergeant, you'll find out that these two were on that lugger. When they don't show up it will be assumed that they drowned. Right?"

"That's right, Mr. Cuomo." Sergeant Hummock looked at Sandy and David and shook his head. "I warned you to stay away. You wouldn't listen. Now it's too late."

"I don't — " David's voice broke. He cleared his throat and tried again. "I don't understand. What's going on?"

"You don't have to understand. We've got a

good thing going here and you're a threat to it. You have to be put out of the way."

"Look," snapped the yachtsman impatiently, "you have to make sure they're never found. Either that or make sure it looks like drowning. Which is it?"

"Either way," broke in Cliff Turner, "it's not your problem.

"Look, Cuomo, as far as you're concerned you collided with an unidentified boat. You searched for survivors without success. Hummock will vouch for that. You came here to search in case survivors made it this far. Again, nothing. You've done all you could. Now, off you go back home to Oban. Leave these two up to us. Trust me — we'll finish this off so you're in the clear. I'd advise you not to stop at the cave this time though. Don't forget the *Maisie*'s here. Go straight home."

Mr. Cuomo hesitated, then shrugged. "All right. Let me get away before you — do anything."

He turned and walked away, fast, almost running. They watched him go.

"The cave?" asked David. Anything to stall for time. "What *is* in the cave?"

Cliff Turner was watching the retreating figure. "Heroin," he said, shortly. "A fortune in drugs."

"Yes," said Sergeant Hummock. "A fortune. And you were a threat. You wouldn't listen. What d'you think, Turner? What's the best way to — settle this?"

"Just a minute." Cliff Turner waited until the figure of Mr. Cuomo had disappeared over the hill leading to the jetty.

"Now!" he said. He turned. He removed the gun from David's back, and thrust it hard against Sergeant Hummock's chest. "Sergeant Hummock, I'm arresting you for attempted murder and trafficking in drugs. That'll do for a start." He turned and winked at Sandy and David. "I'm on your side. I have been all along."

20

"I don't understand," said Sandy. "You *did* take our picture — the one of the inside of the cave — and the negative too, didn't you?"

Sandy, David and Cliff Turner were settled in the lounge at Ramshaw Castle, with a pot of tea and a plate of Mrs. McAllister's scones. The tension and fear of the morning had been followed by a long afternoon of paperwork. David and Sandy had gone over their part countless times; at last, they were about to learn the whole story.

"Oh yes, I took them." Cliff Turner propped one knee over the arm of a chair in the castle lounge and swung his foot back and forth. "I did it for your safety. I suppose that doesn't make sense? Let me explain.

"We have to start with the sinking of the *Neptune* two years ago. On the last day of the salvage operations divers — two of them — discovered a fortune in heroin in a waterproof container in one of the cabins. That posed a problem. What were they to do with it? Should they report it — as one of them wanted — or keep it for themselves, and make themselves rich beyond their wildest dreams? They were still undecided when Alec MacAllister interrupted them. One of them knocked him out, and while he was unconscious they decided to hide it on a ledge above high water — one they had already happened to see.

"They soon discovered that it's not as easy as you might think for amateurs to sell drugs on the street. One of them threatened to turn the whole thing over to the cops. The other — Mike Marsh — saw his opportunity during a salvage operation a short time later and arranged a fatal accident. Now he was on his own. He had the fortune to himself. His plan was to leave the bulk of the drugs in the cave and just take out a bit at a time. That way he hoped not to attract too much attention.

"But Mike was making a big mistake. Tony Cuomo was the drug boss on the west coast and he wasn't about to let an amateur muscle in on his territory. To make a long story short he took over the operation. Mike worked for Cuomo until he started to feel he wasn't getting a big enough share. He complained — and ended up under the wheels of a lorry in Glasgow. He lived, but he was crippled for life.

"Cuomo was quite happy with Mike's original

set-up. He left the bulk of the heroin in the cave and took out just what he needed. That was no problem. His yacht was a familiar sight in the Minch. No one asked questions when it sailed in the vicinity of Sgarbeg.

"Except Archie MacDonald. He began to get curious. And you know what happened to him." He paused. Then he said, "That's why I was worried about you two when *you* began to get curious."

"But what — ? How were *you* involved in all this?"

"I'm a detective. I was working under cover. I wormed my way into Cuomo's favour. We had enough on him to put him away, but we had to find out who was his agent in Lewis. That's what I was trying to discover. The day after the *Kittiwake* saw you two going into our cave, Cuomo asked me to keep an eye on you, to make sure you hadn't seen anything that would give his arrangement away.

"I followed you, David, into the photographer's, then into the tearoom. When you left the pictures in the car I had a chance to look through them. There was just the one that showed the upper shelf. I took it and the negative so Sandy wouldn't see it; I figured she might get curious about that object above the tide mark. And I told Cuomo you hadn't seen a thing and he had nothing to worry about. All the same he told me to continue to watch you.

"And it's a good thing I did. The night you went to Callanish I followed you again. I had been to Stornoway (not Barvas, as I said), and when I got back to the castle your car was gone. I hadn't met you on the road so I figured you must have gone the other way — towards Callanish. So I went along, just in case. And when I got to the entrance I saw your car and a police car. I was there for a few minutes, wondering what was going on, when Sergeant Hummock came out through the gate. He said he was just checking up, because there had been the report of a shot, but all he had seen was you two on a romantic walk, and you were all right and he wasn't about to disturb you.

"What actually happened, of course, was that he had followed you and saw an opportunity to scare you good and proper — you were a bit too curious about Sgarbeg for comfort. He might even have intended to finish you off, we'll never know. Anyway, he heard my car coming before he could finish the job. He had no idea I was one of Cuomo's men, nor did I have any idea he was Cuomo's Lewis agent. In fact neither of us knew about the other — for sure — until yesterday when we met out on Sgarbeg looking for you. Anyway I figured you were in no danger at Callanish if the police were on the scene. Besides, I imagined you wouldn't want to be disturbed. That was a glorious moon."

"I don't know what you're talking about," said

Sandy innocently. "And what about Mike Marsh?"

"I figure he came back to blow the whistle on Cuomo, get him back for the way Cuomo treated him. He didn't know Hummock was Cuomo's man. He called him up and said he had a hot tip, asking the sergeant to meet him at the castle. Hummock recogized him, and thought he'd do Cuomo a favour. He listened to what Mike had to say, then suggested they meet at the island early the next day.

"It was an easy matter for Hummock to cosh him one and then arrange it to look like an accident. Mike must have had a hard skull. He lasted until Alec found him, and tried to say who was responsible, but didn't quite make it."

"But why did you hire Alec to go out to Sgarbeg yesterday? Did you know we were going? Did you know about the *White Swan*?"

"I didn't know about it until yesterday morning. You woke me up when you were trying to be so quiet leaving the castle. I followed you in time to see the old lugger pulling away from shore. I dashed back to Stornoway and yanked Alec out of bed and paid him a fortune to take me to Sgarbeg. Then the fog stopped us.

"Sergeant Hummock came by while we were still anchored, waiting for the fog to clear. He said there had been a report of an accident. The *Kittiwake* had run down an unidentified boat, probably a lugger, and he was worried about you two. My first thoughts were for the accident. Had it been intentional? If so, how had the *Kittiwake* known you were on your way? Only later did it strike me as odd that Sargeant Hummock knew you were out there. That's when I began to wonder about him. Not suspect. Just wonder. So I wasn't completely taken by surprise when I found out *he* was Cuomo's agent in Lewis. That's how Cuomo runs his operation. His left hand doesn't know what his right is doing. It works."

"It works all right," nodded David. "And Cuomo kills anyone who gets in his way. It's only thanks to you we weren't more of his victims. But you let him go back to Oban!"

Cliff Turner grinned. "Into the arms of a squad of policemen with enough fire power to blow the *Kittiwake* out of the water if he put up a fight. But he didn't. He was as mild as a lamb. He's going away for a good long stretch."

Cliff swung his leg off the arm of the chair and stood up, rubbing his long upper lip as he looked at the two of them. "A word of advice. You put the Laird of Ramshaw behind bars. Not once but twice. And I understand you thwarted some jewel thieves back in Canada. You escaped with your lives this time. I humbly suggest in the future you curb that curiosity of yours. Next time you might not be so lucky."

"Luck," said Sandy, "had nothing to do with it. But your point is well taken. We learned a lesson.

In future we'll avoid any hint of adventure. Won't we, Davie?"

"Definitely. And we'll keep telling ourselves that. Of course you can't always avoid getting involved — "

"Oh yes you can," said Cliff Turner severely. "If you put your mind to it. Well, I tried." He held out his hand to each of them in turn. "I warned you. That's all I can do." He grinned. "Goodbye. It's been a pleasure."

"Goodbye. And thanks." Sandy bit her lip. "That's rather inadequate, when all you did was save our lives!"

"Thanks are enough," he said. "Just glad I had the chance."

They watched him go, striding away from the castle. Sandy turned to David. "There's just one thing I don't know."

"What's that?"

"When we were floating around in the fog, calling out to each other you called me — something. Remember?"

"Oh yes, I seem to remember. Let's see. It was something Jemmie Macdonald taught me. It's Gaelic, you know."

"Of course I know. But do you know what it means? Did she translate it for you?"

He hesitated, then grinned. "Yes, I know what it means, Sandy *m'eudail*. Do *you* know what it means?"

She turned to him and linked her fingers behind his neck, drawing his face down to hers. "Oh aye, I know, Davie *m'eudail*."

She kissed him.

Robert Sutherland always wanted to be a writer, but knew he needed to make a living first. So he chose to go into printing and bookbinding — to stay as close to books as possible! Robert grew up in Ontario, but his parents were from England and introduced him to English adventure stories and magazines like *Boys' Own* and *Chums Annual*. Scotland, castles, history and the sea became his passions — especially the sea. In fact, water is always an important element in his books. Whether it is the storm-tossed Altantic or a still lake in Algonquin Park, water always means adventure to Robert Sutherland — and the readers of his books!

Property of English Department
St. Peter Catholic High School